Becca

*B*ecca

Carol Duerksen & Maynard Knepp

Illustrations by Susan Bartel

WILLOWSPRING DOWNS

Becca
Book 4 — Jonas Series
Copyright © 1997 by WillowSpring Downs

First Printing, 1997

Printed in the United States of America

Cover and Story Illustrations by Susan Bartel
Page design & layout by C:PROMPT Creations
Hillsboro, Kansas

This story is a fictional account of an Amish family. Names, characters, places and incidents are either imaginary or are used fictitiously, and their resemblance, if any, to real persons, living or dead, is purely coincidental.

Library of Congress Catalog Number 97-60524
ISBN 0-9648525-4-3

Welcome to the Jonas Series!

It began with a dream — a "what if...," a "suppose we write..." It began with the interest friends and family expressed in Maynard's Amish background. He'd tell stories. They'd listen, spellbound. And we'd go home wondering, "Wouldn't it be fun to write a book?"

So, after years of saying it, we finally put some action behind our words. Carol had come across a quote somewhere that said "If you're going to run with the big dogs, you've got to get off the porch." We decided to get off the porch and write that book. *Runaway Buggy* was conceived.

The delivery of *Runaway Buggy* took place under the expertise of another entrepreneurial Hillsboro business called C:Prompt Creations. They took our manuscript and made it look like a book. And they suggested we call *Runaway Buggy* "Book 1 of the Jonas Series." That sounded pretty neat to us, so we did.

Runaway Buggy was released in October 1995, and six weeks later we realized we'd better do a second printing. We also decided to write Book 2 in the Jonas Series, because it appeared that people who'd met our fictional character, Jonas Bontrager, in *Runaway Buggy* wanted to read more. Jonas's life continued in *Hitched,* which was released in August of 1996, and in *Preacher,* which came out in November 1996.

You're now holding the fourth book in the series in your hand. After writing three books from Jonas's perspective, it was fun to "get inside" a teenage girl and to experience the joys and frustrations of Jonas and Sue Ann's oldest daughter, Becca, as she turned 16. We hope you'll enjoy her story.

What's next? The Jonas Series is going to take a "time out" while we begin an offshoot series called the Skye Series. Becca's life will continue in Book 1 of the Skye Series called *Twins*. We're really excited about this book because it will combine some of the characters and settings from the Jonas Series with a new focus and direction. The main story line for *Twins* has been running around in Maynard's head for years, so we're glad for the opportunity to finally do something about it.

The truth of the matter is, we wouldn't be doing any of this if it weren't for you and other readers like you. Self-publishing books is a risky, on-the-edge, yet very rewarding thing for us right now. Thanks so much for your support! It means everything, and as long as you want to read what we write, we'll do our best to keep up our end of the deal.

Carol Duerksen & Maynard Knepp

Contents

Chapter 1

Sixteen

"Under the table, birthday girl! Under the table, birthday girl!" the chant surrounded Becca Bontrager as she forked the last piece of country sausage into her mouth. Her dancing dark eyes laughed at 13-year-old Lydianne beside her, then turned to tease 10-year-old E.J. seated across from her.

"You've got to catch me first!" Becca said, giggling. With a flurry of skirts and bare feet she left the table, her sister and brother in hot pursuit. The screen door slammed behind them as Becca flew out of the house into the early April morning light. Laughing and daring her siblings in the chase, Becca circled the white frame house twice, then entered it again as fast as she'd left. She slid under the kitchen table and sat there, panting and grinning. Lydianne and E.J. ended their chase at the table edge and squatted down to look at Becca.

"You are so weird, Becca," Lydianne blurted somewhat breathlessly. "Why didn't you just go under there in the first place?"

"Because she's Becca, that's why," their father, Jonas, commented from his chair beside the table. He bent down to look at his daughter under the table. "Am I right?" His blue eyes shone with mirth, and a smile spread above his heavy blond beard. Becca's bright eyes and ornery grin met her father's gaze.

"Yeah, but you'd think she'd act more grown up, now that she's 16," Lydianne taunted.

"Sweet 16 and never been kissed!" E.J. joined in.

"And she won't get kissed, 'cause she'll probably run away and say 'You have to catch me first!'" Lydianne said.

Chapter 1

"Well, that's not such a bad idea," their mother, Sue Ann, said, joining the conversation. "I don't mind our girl being a little hard to catch, do you, Dad?"

"No siree! Not at all!" Jonas said, laughing.

"Hello! Have I been here long enough?" Becca asked, peering out from underneath the table. "Have I fulfilled my birthday obligation to everyone's complete satisfaction?" she inquired. For as long as she could remember, whoever was having a birthday in their family got put under the table. The lighthearted family tradition went back to her father's family — why, she'd even seen her grandpa and grandma sitting under the table on their birthdays! Jonas had brought the tradition along with him when he got married and started a family of his own.

"Woo woo woo! Where'd you get all those big words?" E.J. asked, breaking into Becca's thoughts. "I'm only ten, you know. How am I 'sposed to understand all of your fancy talkin'?"

"Sure you can get up," Sue Ann answered her daughter, then turned to her son. "And she probably knows those words because she reads a lot. Something you could afford to do a little more of, from the looks of your last report card. And speaking of ... are you ready to leave for school? You too, Lydianne. It's almost time."

"I'm ready," E.J. said. "What's for lunch?" he asked, picking up his red Coleman lunch box from the kitchen counter, then taking his Amish straw hat off its hook and plopping it on his straight blond hair.

"It's a special surprise lunch!" Sue Ann replied, smiling

at her son. "Now you two be careful and watch the factory traffic. See you after school!"

"Bye!" Jonas added, standing up from the table and walking to the window. He watched as E.J. and Lydianne strode out the lane and down the sand country road. They had about a mile to walk to reach their school. It wasn't a bad walk — the only part that worried Jonas and Sue Ann was the short stretch of road near the school that had a lot of heavy traffic from people going to work in the local mobile home factory.

"Looks like a beautiful day," Jonas noted, watching the sunrise streak the Kansas clouds and sky in pinks, blues and yellows. "A good wash day for you women, and a good day for me to do some field work."

"Can I come help you with the field work?" Becca asked, walking up to stand beside her father.

"It's wash day. Aren't you helping Mom?"

"It doesn't *have* to take two people."

Becca watched as Jonas looked to Sue Ann for an answer. Becca knew she was wishing for more than she could hope to happen. Helping put the family laundry through the hand-operated wringer-washer and hanging it all out to dry — that was her job as a woman. Sure, she'd done field work before too, but never on wash day.

"Please? Just today?" she begged. "As part of my birth-day present?"

Sue Ann smiled at her daughter. "Don't you think, with you getting older and ready to date — which could in fact lead to marriage someday — you should be learning more about housework and spending less time with the horses and stuff outside?"

Becca's mouth turned up in a slight pout. "I'm going to find myself a husband that likes to do the laundry, and I'll work with the horses."

"Oh!" exclaimed Sue Ann, her dark eyes twinkling. "And I suppose he's going to have the babies too!"

"Be fine with me," Becca laughed, and her parents joined in.

Chapter 1

"Looks to me like you've got quite a hunt ahead of you," Jonas chuckled. "Anyway, about you helping with the field work," he looked at his wife as he spoke, "if it's okay with Mom, you can do the springtoothing today. That way I can go into Wellsford and get some corn to plant. What do you think, Sue Ann?"

The sound of a crying baby broke into the conversation.

"Sounds like Emma is awake," Sue Ann said. "Becca, why don't you go get her up and dressed. Then you can go work with Daddy today, but just today. Because it's your birthday. We're not going to make a habit out of this, okay?"

"Okay!" Becca grinned broadly, her white teeth flashing in her naturally dark complexion. Her chocolate brown eyes danced with mischief and fun. "Promise! I won't ask again! At least not until next Monday!"

Becca's whole body shook as she rode standing on the springtooth pulled by the team of Belgians. The rumps of the four huge draft horses plodded along in front of her as the horses methodically worked their way through the brown Kansas soil. Controlling a team of horses was no small feat, and not all Amish girls would dare try. Many of them wouldn't want to. But Becca had always been a tomboy, preferring to work outdoors with the horses and other farm animals than inside learning domestic chores. This resulted in a tenuous compromise with her parents. She agreed to help Sue Ann and was picking up the basics of sewing, cooking, canning, and keeping house — the essentials for any Amish woman — even though her heart wasn't in it. Her heart was outside, and the fact that she was the oldest child, and six years older than her brother, worked to her advantage. She could help her father with things E.J. was still too young to handle. But those things were getting fewer and fewer, and that scared Becca. She didn't want to be replaced.

Chapter 1

The team was pulling the springtooth up a slight hill, and when they reached the top, Becca could see the Wellsford grain elevator in the distance. Wellsford might provide an answer to her potential dilemma, she reasoned. She'd get a job in town. Maybe at the Deutchland Restaurant, where her mother had worked before she got married. She'd be a waitress. Sure, she'd have to bring her money home to her parents, but it would be a lot better than sitting at home doing laundry and taking care of Emma all of the time.

Not that she didn't like her little sister. Emma was a sweetheart. At nine months, she was starting to show her personality more and more, and the family doted on her. She got a lot of attention, too, because there weren't any other children between her and 10-year-old E.J. It made sense for Lydianne to help with Emma while she got a job in town, Becca figured.

The horses liked going down the hill much better than going up, and soon they were at the end of the small field. Becca concentrated on the four separate reins in her hands, her strong fingers straining to guide the horses into the turn. "Gee!" she yelled firmly. "Gee, John! Gee, Paul! Gee, George! Gee, Ringo!" The Belgians responded dutifully, turning to the right, then right again, and began working their way back up the hill. Becca grinned. She loved working with "the Beatles," as she and her father laughingly called the team. Jonas had purchased them at an auction — the former owner hadn't been Amish. "One of those '60s guys who loved the Beatles, a simple lifestyle, and whatever it was he was growing on his land" was the way Jonas described the horses' former owner. At any rate, he'd named the big sorrel Belgians after the Beatles. The Bontragers were used to it by now, but the names still drew chuckles and sideways glances from other Amish folks when they heard them, especially since her father was a minister in the church. "There goes preacher Jonas Bontrager and the Beatles," the people would say.

I wonder what their music sounds like, Becca thought to herself. Guess I'll be able to find out soon, now that I'm 16. I'm sure someone in the young folks has one of their CDs. Although that's not what they're listening to. It's country or rock. This is going to be fun, running around with the young folks. I wonder when I'll start … maybe in a couple of weeks. Or a month. There are a few other girls turning 16 pretty soon. Maybe we'll start together. Becca's heart fluttered, and her stomach twitched. Yes, it'd be fun. But it would be so different. And what if guys started paying attention to her? She blushed involuntarily under the wide Kansas sky.

Becca drove the team home late that afternoon. Stopping them in the yard near the barn, she told E.J., who was feeding the bucket calves, to tell their father the team was ready to be unhitched. Hitching and unhitching the four draft horses was more than she had tackled by herself. She'd go in and take her father's place in the dairy barn while he took care of "the Beatles."

Lydianne was in the milk parlor when Becca entered the barn. "Did you have fun?" Lydianne asked, wiping down a cow's udder before putting the milking machine on.

"Yep, I did," Becca said. "I wish I had a birthday every Monday. By the way, who all's coming over tonight?"

"What do you mean?"

"I mean who all's coming over? Both sides of the family? Or one tonight and one another time?"

"What are you talking about?" Lydianne asked, looking at her sister innocently.

"Lydianne, look me straight in the eyes and tell me nobody's coming over tonight for my birthday. Go ahead!"

"I've gotta go on to the next cow," Lydianne said, scooting past Becca. "Besides," she flung back as she walked by, "what makes you think you're so important that everybody's coming over for your birthday?"

The words were no more out of Lydianne's mouth than a stream of warm milk hit her squarely on the seat. She grabbed her dress and spun around to see Becca busily wiping a cow's teat.

"Becca! You stop it!" Lydianne screamed. "You are so...!"

"Girls, girls, girls!" Sue Ann chided as she stepped into the barn, Emma on her hip. "What have you found to argue about this time?"

"She shot milk at me," Lydianne accused.

"I just asked her who's coming over tonight and she got all smart-alecky with me," Becca countered. "Who's coming, Mom?"

"And if I don't answer, do I get a shot of milk too?" Sue Ann's brown eyes could tease as easily as Becca's. Becca looked at her mother and then her sister. She couldn't take being kidded as easily as she could give it out.

"Well, since nobody seems to know of anything going on here tonight, maybe I'll go for a nice long horseback ride after the chores are done," Becca said.

"Suit yourself," Sue Ann laughed lightly at her oldest daughter. "If we do happen to have some birthday cake, we'll save a piece for you."

❖ ❖ ❖

Chapter 1

Becca sat on her bed later that evening, re-reading her birthday cards. She'd been right, of course. Both sides of the family had filled their house with children, food and fun that evening.

They'd had a great time together. And the presents — what fun! A pretty new lamp for her bedroom — with lavender oil in it! Her mother must have told the rest of the family that she was using lavender and white in her bedroom, because she got quite a few gifts with those colors. She'd been almost speechless when she opened the large garbage bag and pulled out a beautiful white quilt—white with dainty little lavender flowers painstackingly hand embroidered on it. One look around the room revealed whose hours of time had gone into it — Grandma Bontrager couldn't hide her smile of happiness at Becca's exclamations of joy.

But there was another present that just blew her away — one so unexpected and yet so incredible. She'd opened a plain white envelope, thinking she'd find a birthday card. Instead, it contained a picture she recognized immediately as the one she'd had on her dresser for years — a picture of a big black horse named Preacher. Preacher had been a part of their family when she was a young girl, until her father sold him to a racing stable when Becca was 8 years old. Her father had asked their "English" friend and neighbor Cindy Jacobs to take a picture of the horse for Becca to keep as a remembrance. Cameras and picture-taking were taboo among the Amish, but Jonas had decided it was okay for Becca to have a picture of her favorite horse.

She'd cried and cried when Preacher left, and his picture had been on her dresser ever since. At least until her parents "borrowed" it.

Becca held the picture up to the lantern light, and re-read the note taped to the back of it. Her heart skipped a beat just like it had earlier when she read it for the first time.

Chapter
1

"Remember Preacher?" the note read. "You'll get to go see him in Indiana the next time a ride is going that way, and when it works out for you to be gone for a few days. Happy Birthday! Love, Mom and Dad."

Becca turned the picture over and smiled at the tall stallion. Preacher! She was going to Indiana to see Preacher!

Chapter 2

Town Day

Becca'd been anticipating the trip into Wellsford ever since the day after her birthday, when her mother told her they'd be going the next Tuesday. "We'll buy material for some dresses for you," Sue Ann had said. "We'll get groceries, go to the hardware store, make a day of it." It all sounded great to Becca. Anything to relieve the boredom of domestic chores at home.

The morning of their "town day" dawned wet and windless. At 5:00 a.m., when Becca went outside to help with the morning milking, her flashlight beam diffused in a heavy curtain of fog. I know what Dad'll say when I get into the barn, Becca thought. "Looks like we'll have a lot of rain 90 days from now." One of those Amish weather wisdoms of his that he always says.

Becca stepped into the barn. The bright light of Coleman lanterns hanging on the wall greeted her, along with the sounds and smells of dairy cows. The cows stood in two rows, and Jonas was starting to wash their teats.

"Morning, Becca," Jonas greeted her cheerfully. "And a foggy one it is. Guess we'll have us a good rain about 90 days from now."

"You know, Dad, one of these days I'm going to hold you to that," Becca replied, starting down the second row of cows with the teat wash. "I'm going to write it down on the calendar and check up on you."

"You go right ahead," Jonas said, chuckling. "And get your rubber boots ready to walk in the mud."

Lydianne appeared in the barn shortly, and the three milked the family's Holstein cows in about two hours. When they emerged from the barn around 7:00, the gray blanket of fog still hung, dripping, over their farm. Somewhere behind it a sun was shining, but it had made little progress in breaking through.

Chapter 2

"Lotsa rain," Jonas predicted and winked at Becca as they walked toward the house. "You mark it down."

"Kinda spooky out here, isn't it?" Sue Ann commented to Becca as they left the yard in their buggy two hours later. "I sure thought the fog would have lifted by now."

"Me too," Becca agreed. She was seated beside her mother in the front seat of the buggy, holding baby Emma. "It's hard to see much of anything out here. Do you think it scares Dottie?"

"I don't think so. She's an experienced horse. She's seen fog before. I'm more worried about people seeing us."

"Yeah," Becca stared into the grayness around them. A car could come upon them so quickly and not have time to stop before hitting the slow-moving horse and buggy. She decided not to think about it.

"So what kind of material are we going to get for my dresses?" she asked.

"Oh, I guess you'll have to look at it," Sue Ann responded. "Plus we'll get some elastic for the waist, and buttons and zippers. I thought maybe on the way back we could stop at Katie Beachy's and pick up one of Treva's dresses for a pattern. I want something to look at when I make yours."

Becca smiled to herself. The dresses her mother would be making signified that she was of dating age. Running with the young folks. The dresses could have fancier collars and sleeves, and elastic around the waist. A few little touches here and there would make the dresses just a little bit more attractive, more complimentary of the maturing young body inside of them. And of course, not having to pin everything — well that was worth a whole lot by itself.

"Why do girls and women have to use straight pins in our dresses?" Becca asked, wondering out loud.

"I have no idea," Sue Ann answered, then continued, "I guess it's because we've always done it that way. Because buttons and zippers are showy. Worldly. I don't know. It's just what we do."

"It's the same answer for everything, isn't it," Becca observed, staring ahead at the rump of the horse in front of them. The clop-clop-clop of Dottie's shoes on the road was a familiar, almost comforting sound.

"You might say that," Sue Ann agreed.

"Don't you ever ask questions? Don't you ever wonder why?"

"Your father and I have been through that stage. On our own, and together. We asked a lot of questions when we were teenagers. And then, when we were going to join church and get married, we had to decide whether to go with the horses church or the tractors. That wasn't easy at all."

"How did you decide?"

"We couldn't see any biblical reason for one or the other. My family was with the tractors, and his family was staying with horses. Either way, somebody was going to be upset. We finally decided to stay with the horses because we somehow felt horses were safer for our children to be around."

"That's how you decided?"

"Becca, some things don't have easy answers. And some things we make more complicated than they really are. We had to make a decision we could live with, and that's how we did it."

A semi-truck appeared in the fog ahead of them and whizzed past. Dottie flinched and the gush of air pressure pushed against the buggy briefly. Emma squirmed in Becca's arms, and Becca reached into the diaper bag for a bottle of juice. Emma took it in her chubby hands and sucked on it enthusiastically, her blue eyes gazing contentedly at Becca.

Chapter 2

Landmarks weren't easy to see, but when they passed a farm she knew wasn't far from Wellsford, Becca sighed with relief. "Almost there," she said, and Sue Ann nodded.

Wellsford was a medium-sized town surrounded by a community of farmers in central Kansas. Approximately half of those farmers were Amish, and for them, Wellsford was the center of business trade. Grain that they sold went to the Wellsford Co-op, and feed they purchased for their livestock came from there as well. An Amishman owned a buggy shop near the center of town, and the hardware store did a thriving business by catering to the unique needs of the Amish. A bank and a locally owned credit union served the community — in fact, the Wellsford Credit Union had recently built a three-sided shed for the Amish to tie their horses up while they shopped in the downtown area. That was where Sue Ann drove Dottie that morning.

"I guess we'll start at Alice's," Sue Ann said, taking Emma from Becca's arms. Becca jumped down from the buggy, and she and her mother walked toward Alice's Fabrics. "How many dresses did you say we were making?" Becca asked teasingly.

"I was thinking I'd sew one, and then you'd make one," Sue Ann responded.

"I was afraid of that," Becca answered. "Seein's as how sewing is my favorite thing to do, you know."

"Favorite thing or not, you need to do it. How else are you going to clothe yourself and your children someday?"

"I know, I know," Becca said, opening the door to the fabric store.

Thirty minutes later, they emerged from the same door, sacks in hand. They put the sacks in the buggy and walked to the hardware store a block away.

Inside the store, Sue Ann handed Emma back to Becca. "It'd help me out if I didn't have to watch her while I'm shopping," she said.

Becca took Emma and began wandering through the store. Her wandering had a purpose, however. The hardware store was joined by a door to the appliance store next to it. The appliance store had televisions. Amish kids loved coming to the hardware store with their parents.

Becca walked casually into the appliance store and in the direction of the row of televisions, all five of them displaying the same program. The bright screens caught Emma's attention and she pointed at them, a slobbery smile spreading across her mouth.

As near as Becca could figure, some sort of talk show was in process. A teenage girl was yelling at what could be her mother. The words on the screen under the girl said "Wants to have a baby at age 14." Becca stood transfixed at the conversation. Why would anyone want to have a baby at 14? The girl wasn't married. She just wanted a baby. It didn't make sense.

Afraid her mother would be done shopping and come looking for her, Becca walked back into the hardware store.

Sue Ann had just stepped up to the cash register. Perfect timing, Becca thought to herself.

"Anything good on TV?" Sue Ann deadpanned as they

walked out of the hardware store. Becca looked at her mother, a guilty grin crossing her face.

"Actually, no," she answered. "Some 14-year-old girl was telling her mother she wanted to have a baby. She wasn't even married or anything. It all seemed kinda stupid to me."

"Yeah, well, there's a lot of stuff going on in the world that isn't good or right," Sue Ann said. "Just think, if we had a TV in our house, you'd be watching that kind of stuff all the time."

Becca didn't answer. She'd never really thought about it that way. She knew the Amish didn't have televisions because they didn't have electricity, and televisions were worldly and unnecessary. But they were also very interesting and appealing.

The sun had finally chased away the dreary fog and a gorgeous April day was in the making as they walked back to the buggy.

"You want to drive?" Sue Ann asked as she untied the horse from the hitching post.

"Sure," Becca agreed. Driving Dottie, even in town, was usually a breeze compared to handling the Beatles.

"I'm getting hungry. Can we go eat?" Becca asked, turning Dottie out of the credit union parking lot.

"Yeah, it must be about that time," her mother agreed. "Where shall we go?"

"Let's go to the Deutchland Restaurant and you can tell me about when you worked there and started dating Daddy," Becca said.

"Oh that was a long time ago."

"But you remember it — I know you do. You've told us about it before."

"Then I don't need to tell you again."

"Yes, I want to hear all the *juicy* details. Stuff you

haven't told us when Lydianne and E.J. were listening. I'm 16 now, so I should know."

"Becca, Becca, Becca," Sue Ann said, laughing. "That's what scares me."

Within minutes Becca was turning Dottie into the parking lot of the Deutchland Restaurant and up to the hitching post. She jumped out to tie the horse, and took Emma from her mother so Sue Ann could get out of the buggy.

"So, has this place changed since you worked here?" Becca didn't waste any time broaching the subject after they'd ordered their food. Emma sat in a high chair between them, banging a spoon against the tray.

"Not much. I don't know if the waitresses are as good as they were then," Sue Ann teased, her dark eyes twinkling mischievously.

"I'm sure they aren't," Becca agreed and laughed lightly. "Did you like being a waitress?"

"Actually, I did. I liked the contact with the people."

"I've heard Dad say you flirted with the guys who came in," Becca teased.

"If you're going to listen to your dad talk about me flirting with guys, then you should ask him to tell you about Debbie, too," Sue Ann said, handing Emma a bottle.

"Who's Debbie?"

"Debbie is Harlan Schmidt's daughter. She has a family of her own now and lives in Kentucky, but he dated her for awhile, when he first started working at the Schmidt dairy."

"Really? How long?"

"Oh, I'm not sure. Not real long. He broke up with her after one of our Amish young folks, Enos, got killed."

"Is that the guy that got shot in Vicksburg?"

"Yes."

The waitress brought their food, and in between

mouthfuls of fried chicken and mashed potatoes and gravy, Becca continued her questioning. She loved hearing about her parents during their teenage years, and the thought that she would soon be running with the young folks and dating made it even more exciting.

"So how did you and Dad get together?"

"We were good friends, even when we were dating other people. I was dating an Amish guy who decided he wasn't going to stay Amish, and I broke up with him because I knew I wanted to stay. After Jonas stopped dating Debbie, we started going out. In fact, you know when I knew he was really interested in me?"

"When?" Becca asked, leaning forward eagerly.

"When he chose to take me to a Garth Brooks concert instead of taking Debbie. He'd even gotten the tickets from her parents, but he took me!"

"Really?"

"Yeah," Sue Ann said, smiling as she remembered. "And you know what I did for him in return?"

"What?"

"We stopped at a western store on the way to the concert and I bought him a black cowboy hat. Oh my, did he look good in that!"

Becca giggled and tried to imagine her father as a teenager, wearing a cowboy hat. It was hard to do. His beard and Amish haircut was so much a part of him — it was the only way she knew him. And she'd never seen pictures of him any other way.

"Did Dad have a car?"

"No, he borrowed the Schmidt's pickup."

"If he got used to driving their pickup and you went to concerts and stuff, did you ever think of leaving?"

"The Amish? Sure, we considered it, on our own, at different times. But we both came to realize that this is what we are meant to be, and it's the only way we'll be happy. Very few people leave, and I have yet to see anyone who seemed to really have his act together. And I say 'his' because if anyone does leave, it's more often a guy than a girl."

"Why?"

"I'm not sure. Except maybe they have more opportunities. They buy cars. They get good-paying jobs in factories. Things like that."

"Yeah, I guess that makes sense," Becca said thoughtfully.

"Would you ladies like some dessert?" their waitress wanted to know.

"No, thank-you, " Sue Ann answered. "Emma's getting antsy, so we'd better be going. Besides," she added after the waitress was out of earshot, "I was thinking we'd stop at McDonald's before we go home and get ice cream cones."

"Sounds good to me," said Becca, pushing away from the table.

The only thing between them and McDonald's was a big grocery shopping excursion. Becca was glad they weren't in a van with a group of women going shopping because then they'd have to wait on everyone. This way, when they were done they could leave.

By two o'clock Becca was driving Dottie out of the grocery store parking lot, the back of the buggy loaded with several weeks' worth of food staples. The Golden Arches weren't far away.

Becca stopped Dottie at the drive-through menu and asked for two ice cream cones.

"Get a spoon so I can give Emma some," Sue Ann reminded.

An ornery idea crossed Becca's mind, and she started chuckling quietly.

"Watch this," she said to her mother. She clucked with

her mouth at Dottie, and the mare walked forward a short distance. Just when her head was even with the drive-through window, Becca pulled back on the reins. "Whoa, Dottie," she commanded, still giggling.

It didn't take long for the window to open, and although Becca couldn't see the person inside, she could imagine the look on his or her face. Someone had been prepared to hand an ice cream cone out to a person driving a car, and had instead been confronted with a large horse's head. Becca laughed out loud as she clucked at Dottie again, and the horse pulled up a few more feet before Becca stopped her. Becca looked into the window, and met the eyes of a woman about her mother's age. She looked tired, but she was smiling.

"I gave the ice cream to the horse," the woman said. "Did you order something too?"

Later that evening, after the family had eaten together and everyone had laughed at the story of Dottie's ice cream, after doing the dishes and playing with Emma, after helping E.J. with his homework, and after trying on the dress they'd picked up from Treva Beachy, Becca retired to the room she shared with Lydianne. It'd been a full, fun day — one that had started at 5:00, as all her days did. By 9:00 she was ready for bed. Tomorrow they'd start sewing her first dress, because she wanted to have both of them to take along to Indiana. She didn't know yet when that would happen, but she wanted to be ready.

Becca stood in front of her dresser, the light from the lantern throwing shadows against the wall. Reaching up to her white covering, she took the pins out that held it to her head, then lifted the stiff covering off and set it on the dresser. She stared at her dark hair pulled back behind her head, twisted in a braid, and tied at the back of the head. It wasn't smooth and sleek like her mom's. No, her hair waved and curled and danced. It hated being tied back. She undid the knot in the string holding it back, and the heavy braid dropped down. Then she let the braid unravel.

Totally unmanageable, she sighed. Curls and silliness everywhere! She grabbed her hairbrush and began brushing. A hundred strokes a day, somebody had said. Well, what's the point of brushing it all out just to stick it under a covering again the next morning, she thought, as she'd thought many times before. "Someday, your husband will love your beautiful hair," her mom had told her. Which was all fine and good, Becca figured, except that the only time he'd get to see it down was when she washed it and when they went to sleep.

She stopped the brushing and stared again. It changed her whole appearance, having her hair down. Now her dark eyes and slightly rounded face were framed in hair, hair everywhere. Hair that wanted to bounce and fly. Hair that frizzled with freedom and giggled with fun at being loose and out. Like her mom kept saying, hair that had a life of its own.

How would it feel to have her hair down when she went someplace? She smiled nervously at herself in the mirror. Now that she was 16, she'd start running with the young folks. And she'd let her hair down.

Did it make her pretty? Debatable, she decided. Not pretty like her mom. She'd seen pictures of her mom as a teenager, "illegal" pictures taken before she joined the church. She was beautiful, and her hair was so perfect.

On the other hand, there was something about the rebelliousness of her hair that Becca liked. It conformed to the covering when it had to, all right, but when let out — look out! Surprisingly enough, Lydianne had even said she looked good with her hair down. "It's you," she had commented. Whatever that meant.

Chapter 3

Saturday Night

Agirl didn't want to look too anxious, but neither did she want to appear square and wait forever to get started, Becca knew from talking to other teenagers. She had to decide when her first weekend out with the young folks would be. The last weekend in April seemed right. She told her mother while they were working on her dresses.

"You know there are some kids that are good to be with, and others that are troublemakers," Sue Ann warned as she peddled the sewing machine in their sunny east porch.

"Yeah, I know," Becca said out loud, and the phrase echoed in her head. I know, I know, I know.

"Some of the guys with the hot pickup trucks, like Al and Stuart. They drive like crazy, and I don't want you riding with them."

"Yes, Mother," Becca said, not looking up from the dress she was hemming.

"It's just that I'm worried about accidents."

"Yes, Mother."

"So you aren't going to ride with them?"

Becca didn't answer.

The sewing machine stopped.

"Becca, I'm not trying to be hard on you. And I know you're going to make your own decisions no matter what I say. But I can't help myself. I'll probably worry about you from now until you join church and get married."

"Please! I haven't even gone out yet and you're getting ready to worry from now until kingdom come!"

Sue Ann fiddled with the dress and moved it around. The sewing machine started again.

"You're right, but I guess that's what mothers do."

"I'll take care of myself, Mom."

"And what will you do when everyone else is drinking?"

"I don't know."

"You might want to think about that before you're in that situation. Or what about if the guy you're riding with has been drinking?"

"Look, Mom. I know better than to ride with somebody who's been drinking."

"I hope so."

"Is this the end of the lecture?" Becca didn't hold back the "I'm-tired-of-this" sarcasm in her voice. She looked at her mother. Hurt hung in her face. The sewing machine slowed to a stop, and Sue Ann pulled the dress out from under the sewing foot. She handed it to Becca.

"It's ready for the hem," she said flatly as she stood up and left the porch.

You'd think my goal in life is to do everything I can to destroy myself and make her worry, Becca grumbled within herself. I'm not stupid.

Becca did admit to herself, however, that she worried a bit about who would pick her up that first night. The guys would decide among themselves who would go get her and bring her to wherever the group was gathering for the evening. She hoped it wasn't one of the older guys — she'd feel so young and naive compared to them. But she didn't want one of the "simmies" either. A simmy was a guy who'd just turned 16, and she'd gone to school with all of those guys. Still a bit immature, as far as she was concerned. Oh well, she'd just have to wait and see.

When that Saturday evening finally did arrive, and a horse and buggy careened into their yard, Becca was relieved to see that it was Vern Yoder's rig. She knew all of the guys' buggies by the different arrangements of reflectors on the front and back. Vern's white reflectors made a circle around his back window.

"Have fun!" Lydianne yelled as Becca whizzed through the kitchen on her way out.

"Be careful!" Sue Ann added.

Becca paused at the door and grinned at both of them. "I will," she said, winking at Lydianne. Then she turned to her mother and said, "And I will!"

The door slammed behind her, and she ran lightly toward the waiting buggy.

"Hi!" the curly-haired young man said as Becca hoisted herself into the buggy.

"Hi, Vern," Becca replied as she sat down beside him. Her eyes traveled from his reddish-gold hair down to his obviously store-bought shirt, blue jeans and cowboy boots. Vern was 17 and had been running with the young folks for a year. She couldn't have done better if she'd picked someone herself, Becca thought. She couldn't help but smile with pleasure and excitement.

Vern slapped the reins across his horse's back and they rumbled down the lane and onto the road.

"Pretty dress," Vern complimented. Obviously, he'd been checking her out too. She was glad she'd worn the lavender one.

"Guess you're about the first one to see it," Becca said, giggling self-consciously. "Don't look too close — I hate to sew."

"Looks fine to me," Vern said, grinning down at her.

"So, what's happening tonight?" Becca asked.

"Oh, we'll all meet at the Star Bowl for awhile, and then go from there," Vern answered.

"Don't tell me I'm going to have to bowl for the first time in my life, in front of everyone."

"Oh, we'll see. It's not like it's the only 'first' you're going to have," Vern said teasingly.

Becca blushed. She could imagine what he was talking about.

"Bowling's not so bad," Vern said, and Becca was glad he'd gone back to a less embarrassing topic. "You just roll a ball down the lane and with a little luck, you'll knock some pins down. You're athletic. You can do it."

"We'll see."

"We're all terrible, really. But it's fun."

Their conversation continued as they drove into Wellsford, and Becca was glad Vern was so easy to talk to. He turned his horse into the parking lot of Star Bowl, and he automatically walked up to the hitching post. Vern jumped out, tied him up, and the two walked into the bowling alley.

Becca felt as though everyone was looking at her when they walked in, and she felt her face turning red. A group of Amish kids had already claimed one of the lanes, a few more were playing pool and just hanging around. Other than the fact that she knew them, it wouldn't have been easy to identify them as Amish by their appearance. Except for one or two other girls in dresses — friends of hers who had also recently turned 16 — everyone was wearing "English" clothes. She'd left home feeling great in her new "dating dress," but she was already starting to wish for some jeans and a T-shirt. She headed toward the girls her age.

"Hi, Becca," a petite girl in a light blue dress greeted her. "Did you have a good ride in with Vern?"

Becca flashed a smile and nodded. "It was okay. Who'd

you come with?"

"Al. That was a wild ride!" Linda exclaimed, rolling her eyes. "But he sure does have a nice pickup! And you know what he told me?" Linda's voice dropped almost to a whisper. "He said he's thinking about makin' a trip up to Indiana sometime soon. He said he might throw a topper on the back of his truck and take a bunch of kids along. Would that be fun or what?"

"Did he ask you to go along?" Becca asked, her eyes wide with surprise. Al was 20 years old, and to be inviting a 16-year-old girl, well, that was quite something.

Linda nodded. "As good as. He said he'd take whoever wanted to go. 'Including you and Becca and Janette.' That's what he said. So you're invited too."

"Oh my!" was all Becca could say.

"Well, girls, shall we do some bowling?" A smooth male voice approached them from behind. Becca and Linda turned to see Al grinning at them crookedly. He was holding up a pair of worn red and green bowling shoes. "Aren't they sweet?" He flipped one up in the air and caught it. "And now, you too, can have a beautiful pair chust like mine!" In typical Amish fashion, his "j" came out "ch," but neither of the girls noticed.

What Becca did notice was that he certainly did fit the description "tall, dark, and handsome." And he smelled so good! Whatever aftershave or cologne he had on, it worked. She blushed slightly, but her eyes met his directly. "So, how do I get myself such a pair of *special* shoes? And do they have to be that *big*?" she asked, feigning naivete and disgust.

"Right this way, young lady, to some shoes chust your size," Al replied as he beckoned her to follow him to the counter.

Moments later, Becca found herself in a foursome on a bowling lane — Al, Vern, Linda and her. The guys' instructions on how to get the heavy ball to roll right down the lane left Becca only more confused, so she decided she'd just watch and do it her own way. When her turn came, she strode up to the marked starting points, flicked her covering strings behind her with one hand while holding the speckled black ball in the other, and then took aim. Three smooth steps later she let go and the ball rolled straight — straight down the lane toward the nine pins. Becca and the other three watched in amazement as all the pins fell without a falter. Becca jumped, her dress twirling around her as she walked back to her shocked friends.

"STRIKE! You did a strike just like that!" Vern exclaimed, glaring at her with his hands on his narrow hips. "Is this beginner's luck or what?"

"I'm sure it is," Becca said, her dark eyes dancing with delight. "Or maybe I'm just good. Who knows?"

Whatever it was, it stayed with Becca through the whole game. Her score was second only to Al's, and that by only a few points.

"You're a natural," Al complimented, admiration in his gray-green eyes. "I am truly impressed."

"It's probably the shoes," Becca joked in return. Her first night out, the attention of two good-looking guys, an impressive bowling score — yes, she could handle this. Running with the young folks was going to be a lot of fun.

"Then what happened?" Lydianne asked breathlessly in the darkness of the girls' bedroom the next evening.

"Nothing," Becca's voice betrayed her little lie.

"Don't tell me that! What happened?"

Becca had already told her younger sister about bowling with Vern, Al, and Linda, and about her good scores. She'd told her about going out for pizza, and how some of the guys had ordered beer. She'd told Lydianne that she had ridden with Vern, Janette, and her date to Janette's home, and how they'd all stayed outside and talked for a long time before going inside for the night.

"BECCA!" Lydianne insisted. "Did he kiss you?"

"Okay, okay, yes, he did," Becca conceded, giggling. "Now are you satisfied?"

Lydianne giggled in return. "No, the question is, were *you* satisfied?"

"It was nice."

"BECCA! Did you get *schnitzeled*?"

"Oh, is that what it was?" Becca asked teasingly. She knew good and well what her sister was getting at. Being *schnitzeled* was the traditional way of initiating a 16-year-old into the dating world. The kissing episode ended with the young couple either talking into the wee hours of the morning or simply falling asleep.

"I know you did, and I'm going to tell Mom and Dad if you don't outright admit it to me," Lydianne threatened.

"And I will make sure I report everything to them when you start running around too," Becca responded.

"Or we could agree not to ever tell on each other," Lydianne suggested quickly.

"We could," Becca said, her eyes getting heavy. "I'm about to fall asleep. I didn't get much sleep last night, you know."

"Yeah, I know. *Sweet dreams!*"

Chapter 4

Nice Guy

Five o'clock came entirely too early for Becca that Monday morning, but she dutifully got up and trudged through the morning chores. The sky was starting to show promise of a sunrise much earlier than it had in the winter, Becca realized. That was a good sign. If only she wasn't so tired. By the time breakfast was over, she was ready for a long nap, but it was, after all, Monday. Wash day.

Becca started the gasoline-powered motor that pumped water through their house. She hooked a hose from the propane water heater to the gasoline wringer washing machine, and filled the tub with hot water. After adding a cupful of homemade lye soap, she dropped the first load of laundry into the steaming water in the round tub, poked it all down with a strong pine stick, and closed the lid.

Ten minutes later, she lifted each piece of clothing out of the hot water and fed it into the wringer part of the machine. A person couldn't be daydreaming or half-asleep during this part, because the wringer could catch a person's hand before she knew it. Becca hated this part the most. Even in cold weather, she'd rather be hanging clothes outside than doing the washing inside. She rather be doing most anything outside than working indoors.

The outdoors part of doing the family wash finally came, and Becca lugged a big basket of wet clothes out to the washline. It was a gorgeous day — 70 degrees, sunny, and very little wind. And it was the last day in April, which meant the month of May should be nice too. Wasn't that what her dad always said? Or was it the last Friday that predicted the next month's weather? She couldn't remember. She'd have to ask him sometime.

And that reminded her of another thing, she thought, clipping a pair of her dad's barn-door pants to the line. Should she talk to her parents about Al going to Indiana and taking a bunch of kids? After all, they'd said a trip to Indiana was her birthday present. But she couldn't fathom her mom letting her ride with Al. No, they'd never let her go. But then, could they stop her?

If she didn't ride with Al, when would she get to go? And with whom? Probably with a bunch of adults. Not nearly as much fun as being in a pickup topper with a group of kids. Surely Al would take the responsibility seriously of driving all those kids. He'd seemed nice enough that evening at the Star Bowl. Her mother was probably overly worried. She'd bring it up at lunch and see what happened.

Jonas was planting corn about a mile away from their farm that day. Rather than driving the team home, or walking home himself, Jonas had suggested that Sue Ann and Becca bring him lunch in the field. That sounded great to Becca — a mile walk on a spring-coming day suited her just fine.

A meadowlark lifted his song above them as Sue Ann and Becca left the lane shortly before noon. Becca pulled a little red wagon with a chortling Emma in it, along with a picnic basket and water jug. Hearing meadowlarks herald spring made Becca feel like singing herself. She loved this time of year, with the outdoors coming alive, and it seemed to put new life in her too. She could almost forget being tired.

The fifteen-minute walk felt good, and Jonas was waiting for them when they got to the field. He'd left the Beatles standing at the end of the field — they wouldn't go anyplace until he told them too — and he was sitting under a tree, watching them walk up.

"Three of the best-looking women in the community, and they come to see me," he said, grinning. "What a lucky fellow I am." He lifted Emma out of the wagon and nuzzled her affectionately.

He's in a good mood, Becca thought to herself. Maybe I'll have a chance to go to Indiana with Al.

Not that her father wasn't usually in a good mood, and he always treated her fairly, she had to admit. But if he'd been having problems with the equipment or something else had gone wrong, it wouldn't have been the best time to bring up the trip to Indiana. The timing looked great today.

Sue Ann and Becca spread the meal out on the blanket Becca had been carrying — big heavy sandwiches filled with homemade canned turkey, carrots, chips, homemade applesauce, and whoopie pies for dessert. The trio bowed their heads in silent prayer, during which Becca heard one of the Belgians snort and shake his head. She also heard a cardinal singing nearby, and the distant sound of a horse's clop-clop-clop on the road. She wondered who it might be, and how close they were. Finally, she sensed Jonas stirring beside her, and knew the prayer was over.

"I haven't heard much about your weekend," Jonas said, opening the conversation. Then he took a huge bite out of his sandwich.

Becca's mouth wrapped around her sandwich, and she chewed awhile before answering.

"It was fun," she summarized after a moment.

"Oh! Well, I'm glad we've got that subject covered," Jonas remarked, his bright blue eyes laughing at his daugh-

ter from under his straw hat. "Or could you possibly fill us in on some of the *details*?"

"We went bowling and out for pizza."

"Mom said it was Vern that picked you up."

"Yeah. He's nice."

Jonas reached for some carrots and glanced at his wife.

"I can tell we're going to hear so much about her weekend, it'll be hard to shut her up and get back to work," he said. Sue Ann smiled and shrugged her shoulders.

"I do have something to talk about," Becca said, her eyes intent on her plate of food. "Al's taking a load of kids to Indiana in two weeks. He's putting a topper on the back of his pickup, and he invited me and Linda and Janette to go," she paused. "And my birthday present was a trip to Indiana…" her voice trailed off.

"What we meant was we'd pay your way to go along with a *safe, adult* driver," Sue Ann responded just like Becca knew she would. "Al hardly meets either of those qualifications."

"I think he'll be careful if he has all of us along," Becca said, trying to sound confident. She could feel her father's eyes on her, studying her, and she could hear him munching on his chips. He was still looking at her when she allowed her eyes to meet his.

"At least I'm asking," she pointed out. "I could have just gone." The threat sounded a little lame, she knew. She knew her parents felt sure she'd tell them before doing something like that. Truthfully, she probably would. But that wouldn't be the case with all of the Amish teens. Especially the older ones.

"Maybe I'll talk to Al," Jonas finally spoke.

"Jonas! What good would that do? I don't trust him!" Sue Ann reacted.

"Honey, we were young once too. Remember?" Jonas

said softly. "At the same time," he said, turning to Becca again, "I do care about your safety."

Becca racked her brain for something to say that would help, but she couldn't find anything. Plainly, her mother was against it and her father wasn't exactly thrilled with the idea.

Chapter
4

"I think Mom and I are going to have to talk about this before we give you an asnwer," Jonas said, reaching for a whoopie pie. A crumb from the chocolate sandwich cookie stuck in his beard as he took a bite, and it didn't dislodge as he savored the sweet dessert.

"Dad," Becca said, reaching toward her father and picking the bit of cookie from his beard, "you saving this for your afternoon snack?" Her brown eyes teased, and a slight smile played around the corners of her mouth.

"Don't mind if I do," Jonas said, picking up on the silliness and reached for another whoopie pie. "You think I could store a whole one there?"

Becca knew better than to bug her parents about their decision. But when she still hadn't heard anything on Saturday morning, her patience wore thin. She'd be with the young folks that evening, and they'd be talking about the trip to Indiana the next weekend. They'd ask if she was going. She needed to know.

The answer came at lunch.

"About your going to Indiana," Jonas addressed Becca. Here it comes, she thought, and noticed that Lydianne and E.J. were suddenly paying very close attention to their father. They knew what was going on, and they were very curious about the outcome too.

"I talked to Al," Jonas continued. "I told him how important you are to me."

A smirk started on E.J.'s face, but one look from his father wiped it off as fast as it appeared.

"I told him how important you are to me," Jonas repeated. "And then I told him I'd really like for you to be able to go to Indiana with him."

Becca's heart skipped with hope. She glanced at her mother, but Sue Ann was pretending to be totally occupied with feeding Emma.

"I told him I know how crazy guys can get when they're driving. I've been there. A bunch of us guys walked away from an accident that wrecked the car and killed a horse," Jonas paused for a moment — just long enough for E.J. to jump in.

"What happened, Dad?"

"We were in Oklahoma for the weekend, and came up over a hill pretty fast. A horse and buggy full of kids was at the bottom of the hill. Our brakes went out, and we plowed into them."

"Were you driving?" Lydianne wanted to know.

"No, Enos was. Anyway, no one was hurt too bad — not us guys or the kids in the buggy. But I'll never forget seeing that horse die — a big black gelding — kinda like Preacher," Jonas looked at Becca when he said the name. "And I'll never forget seeing the guy who owned the horse cry, and how he yelled at Enos that he killed his horse."

The house was quiet. Even Emma seemed to be listening.

"So anyway, I told Al I know guys are going to do dumb things, but I would ask him to refrain when he has the lives of other people in his hands."

"And?" Becca asked impatiently.

"And he said he would. Nice guy, that Al," Jonas concluded.

"So that means I can go?"

"Start packing," Jonas answered. "You've only got a week, you know."

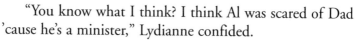

Becca felt like letting out a whoop, but she refrained. One look at her face told the story though.

After lunch, while Becca and Lydianne were washing the dishes, they talked about the decision, and Jonas's conversation with Al.

"You know what I think? I think Al was scared of Dad 'cause he's a minister," Lydianne confided.

"Really?" The idea had never occurred to Becca.

"Yep. I betcha the first thing that came to Al's mind when Dad showed up was 'Uh-oh, here's the minister coming to talk to me.'"

"But that's not how Dad told it."

"He didn't have to say it — not even to Al. But that's how people see him."

Becca thought about it as she dried the plates and stacked them back in the cupboard. If what Lydianne was saying was true, then did the young folks see her differently because she was the daughter of a minister? And would they think her father was using his position to somehow protect her? Worse yet, was she expected to behave a certain way because she was a minister's daughter?

On the other hand, she rationalized, her dad had done wild things as a teenager too. All of the ministers had. So, how could he expect her to be any different?

And Al, was he serious about his response?

"So do you think Al meant what he said, or was he just giving Dad the answer he wanted to hear?" Becca asked Lydianne.

"Hey, don't ask me," Lydianne snorted. "You're the one with the young folks. You go bowling with Al, and all that. *I* don't know Al. What do *you* think?"

"I think he's a nice guy who has to show off," Becca said. "And I think he'll behave himself, at least while driving up there and back. When he's there, that's probably another story."

Chapter 5
Road Trip

Becca silently wished her family had a place to go that second Friday evening in May. She didn't want her parents at home when Al came tearing onto their yard to pick her up. What if, horror of horrors, they'd change their minds about her going to Indiana? No, it'd be better if they weren't around.

But they were. Becca decided to wait in her room, pretending to be doing some last-minute packing. Truth was, she didn't have much to pack for the short weekend away, and she'd rearranged her small suitcase several times already. She was wearing her lavender dress, and the other one — a turquoise blue from the same pattern — was in the suitcase. She smiled as she picked up a pair of new white socks — the kind that folded down and had a neat little stripe along the top. These had a turquoise stripe — a perfect match for the dress. Being a teenager meant being able to wear cute socks with decorations on them. Of course she was wearing the ones with lavendar trim right now. And new sporty-looking white shoes.

"Becca?" her mother's voice came from the doorway. Becca looked up from the suitcase on her bed.

"All packed and ready to leave?" Sue Ann asked.

"Yeah, I think so," Becca said.

"You must be really excited," Sue Ann said flatly, sitting

down on the bed beside the suitcase. Wistfulness and worry seemed laced together in her voice, Becca thought. She sat down on the bed too, on the other side of the suitcase.

"I am, Mom, and I'll be okay," she said, turning the suitcase toward herself and putting the top down.

"I'm sure you will," Sue Ann said, though her hands twisted in her lap. "Sometimes I just can't believe my little girl is 16 and old enough to leave for the weekend. And Indiana seems far away when we go. It seems even farther when you're going with Al and a bunch of kids."

"Didn't you do this when you were a teenager?"

"Yes, I suppose, but this is different."

"How?"

"Now I'm the mom and you're my girl. That's what's different."

Becca stood up and stepped in front of her mother. Leaning down, she silently wrapped her arms around Sue Ann's shoulders and back, and held her close. Becca felt her mother's arms reach out and cling to her, her head with its white covering resting on Becca's chest.

"I love you, Becca," Sue Ann's muffled voice was breaking. "And I pray that God will keep you safe."

"I love you too, Mom," Becca said above her mother's covering.

A motorized rumble began to grow in the distance, and Becca slowly broke the embrace with her mother. "I think I hear Al's truck," Becca said. Please don't do anything stupid, Al, she pleaded internally.

Grabbing her suitcase, Becca hurried out of her room and toward the back door of the house, Sue Ann following behind. Al's shiny red, four-wheel-drive Ford with a much older, used-to-be-white topper slowed down at their lane. In fact, it almost came to a trembling stop before making a perfect left turn onto the yard. Becca watched in amazement as the Ford inched its way toward the house, vibrating with pent-up power.

Stepping outside, Becca noticed her whole family was watching — her dad and E.J. near the barn where they were repairing a piece of equipment, Lydianne and Emma in the garden, and her mother in the door behind her. The strangest thought flashed through Becca's mind. "Curiosity killed the cat" was a phrase she'd heard people say. Well this was as if curiosity had frozen her family in their spots. She reached the back of the pickup, but before opening the door of the topper, she waved in the direction of the barn, then the garden, then the house. "See you later!" she called.

"Bye! Be good!" her father's voice answered.

"Bye, Becca!" E.J. echoed.

"Have fun!" Lydianne encouraged, holding Emma up and helping her wave.

"Be careful," Sue Ann called, a handkerchief in her hand. "Please be careful!"

Becca opened the topper and faced the laughing faces of half a dozen of her friends sitting on pillows and blankets on the pickup bed. She dropped her suitcase in, and then climbed over the tailgate. Al's grinning face appeared in the open sliding window between the cab and topper.

"Am I driving good enough?" he called back with a chuckle.

"Oh, Al, is that you driving?" Becca teased back. "I thought it had to be somebody else."

"Hey, I don't mess around when I'm picking up the minister's daughter," Al responded.

Becca flinched inwardly at the words, but she hadn't detected a bit of derision or sarcasm in Al's voice. Although the other kids were laughing at what seemed to be a light-hearted slam, she didn't see it on Al's handsome face. Instead, he flashed one of his to-die-for smiles, and she melted.

"Well, this minister's daughter is ready to go to Indiana," she managed to say. "What are we waiting for?"

"Your wish is my command," Al said teasingly, turning from the window to the steering wheel. As he slowly backed his pickup out the driveway, Becca could see her family, still frozen in their spots, watching. Her mother's handkerchief was dabbing at her eyes.

Approximately four hours down the road, Al pulled his pickup into a McDonald's parking lot. The seven teens in the topper and the trio in the cab piled out, stretching and shoving each other good-naturedly.

Myrene, one of the girls, said, "Becca, I've got something for you," indicating a plastic bag in her hand. "Let's go to the bathroom."

Inside the McDonald's restroom, Myrene proudly pulled a pair of black jean shorts and white T-shirt out of the bag. "Thought you might want these — sure nicer for traveling, you know," she said, smiling at Becca. "I figured you and I are about the same size, so I brought them for you."

Becca hesitated for a moment, then took the shorts and T-shirt. She knew she'd be wearing English clothes sooner or later. Might as well be now, she thought. And her hair. She should take her hair down too.

Twenty minutes later, the group left the restaurant and converged on the pickup again. The wind tossed Becca's soft tangle of dark hair, and she felt half naked as the warm May breeze hit her bare legs. She felt eyes too, and Becca glanced sideways to see Al looking at her.

"Excuse me, but are you the Becca Bontrager I picked up a few hours ago?" he inquired as he sidled over to her. "It's just that I don't remember those legs."

Becca felt herself blushing, but she refused to let Al get the best of her.

"I don't know what you're talking about," she said, looking down at them, then up at Al. "They're the same legs I had then. You must be seeing things."

Al let out a laugh that carried through the parking lot, then agreed. "I most definitely am," he said. "I most definitely am seeing things."

Between playing cards, telling stories of parties in the past, making faces through the topper's windows at passing cars, listening to music on a boom box and stopping for food, the trip to Indiana went fast. Becca couldn't remember when she'd had so much fun for sixteen hours straight. This was certainly a blast compared to riding with her family or a group of adults in a van.

Early Saturday morning, the pickup roared into the outskirts of Washington County, the largest Amish settlement in Indiana. The first thing Becca noticed was how much more populated this Amish community was compared to hers in Kansas. Houses on little plots of land, and farms on slightly bigger acreages sat side by side for miles and miles. The horizon to horizon open spaces of Kansas didn't exist here. Indiana — at least this part — had more trees and rolling countryside. She was used to seeing the sun come up and go down. Here, although they'd been driving in increasing daylight for more than an hour, she hadn't seen the sunrise. It happened somewhere behind a forest of trees.

Al slowed down as they approached a white frame split-level house set on several acres of perfectly manicured pastures. A small barn was the only other building on the property. Several horses grazed on the lush green grass, still wet with morning dew. Al turned into the short lane, and stopped in front of the house. His face appeared in the window to the topper. He looked tired, Becca thought, but the light hadn't gone out of his eyes as they searched the interior of the topper. Spotting Becca, he grinned.

"Drop-off point for you, Becca," he stated.

"What do you mean?" Becca asked, looking out the window again.

"Your dad didn't tell you? I'm supposed to leave you here with Merv Smuckers until sometime this afternoon. Then I'll be back to pick you up."

No, her dad hadn't told her. Merv Smucker. The man who'd been involved with the sale of Preacher to a racing stable in Indiana. The man who'd know where Preacher was today. Of course. When she'd asked her father how she'd find Preacher once she got to Washington County, he'd told her that Al would help out. What he hadn't said, in his characteristically kind yet fun-loving way, was that he'd secretly made arrangements for her to meet up with Merv to see Preacher.

Becca located her suitcase among the pillows, blankets, paper trash, CDs, and bodies sprawled around the pickup bed, and let herself out of the topper. She thanked Al and walked to the door of the neat white house. She became acutely aware again of her legs, but there was nothing she could do about it now. Merv and his wife were Conservative Mennonites, which meant they weren't as strict as the Amish, but neither did the women wear pants or shorts. Oh well, if her dad had made the arrangements, they'd have to take her in, shorts or no shorts. She rang the doorbell, while Al's pickup idled loudly in the background.

A woman Becca had never seen before came to the door. She was wearing a pink-flowered, homemade dress, and she smiled in a middle-aged pleasant sort of way. "You must be Becca Bontrager. Please come in," she said. Becca turned to wave the pickup on, and stepped inside the house.

"Merv's out feeding the horses, but he'll be in shortly,"

the woman said. "My name's Ella. We're glad to have you here. I'm sure you're tired after the trip up here. Did you get any sleep? Would you like something to drink? Orange juice, maybe? And a shower — I bet you'd like a shower. Just make yourself at home. Come," she said, and started walking toward the kitchen. Becca tagged along like a tired dog on a leash. The woman had just taken over, and Becca didn't know what to do except follow and agree. "Did you say you'd like some juice?" Ella asked.

"Yes, that'd be good," Becca said. "And the shower sounds great too."

"Of course, of course. Merv'll be in soon and we'll have some breakfast together. Then you can clean up, sleep, or go see Preacher — whatever you want to do. Do you have relatives here in Indiana?"

It seemed like forever before Becca heard Merv come in the back door. She was beginning to understand why Merv spent a good share of his time as an "Amish taxi," taking Amish people on trips within the community and from state to state. He probably needed to get away from the prattle prattle prattle of his wife.

"Becca!" She turned toward the familiar voice and saw Merv enter the kitchen. "So glad to see you again!" Merv said, reaching out his hand to shake hers. She didn't remember him being so short. Oh yeah, maybe she'd grown since she saw him last. Anyway, it was the same enthusiastic, friendly Merv.

"My, you've grown a bit since I saw you last," he was saying. "Sixteen now, huh?"

Becca nodded.

"Ah, I could tell you stories about when your dad was running with the young folks," Merv chuckled. "Actually, he was a pretty good kid."

Ella was talking too — Becca didn't catch it all, but she did hear "pancakes or eggs or french toast and of course fried mush."

"Whatever you're having is fine," Becca said in the direction of Ella, and then turned her attention back to Merv.

"So how's Preacher?" she asked.

"He's absolutely great! I'll take you out to see him after breakfast. He's right here, you know."

"He is?"

"Yep. I bought him from Springdale Stables when they quit racing him."

"When was that?"

"About — let me see — five years ago. They decided they didn't want to use him as a stallion, so I bought him, had him gelded, and he's lived here in retirement ever since."

"Do you ever ride him? Or drive him?"

"Sometimes, but not as much as I should. He's getting fat and lazy."

Becca and Merv talked more about his horses, and in no time at all, Ella appeared at the table with a steaming bowl in each hand.

"Breakfast is served," Ella announced, setting the bowls down. "I hope you're hungry, because I've made plenty."

"Hungry" was one thing Becca wasn't. Sleepy, excited, needing a shower — yes, those descriptions fit. But she'd been snacking all night. Hungry she wasn't.

She managed to find room for one pancake and a piece of fried mush. Ella was beside herself, trying to get Becca to eat more, but to no avail. Finally, thankfully, Merv was done eating and said he'd take Becca out to see Preacher.

"I thought you might see him when you drove up, but he was inside waiting for his grain," Merv said as they walked to the new-looking small red barn. "I wonder if he'll remember you."

"Surely not," Becca said, her step quickening. Merv

opened the door and motioned her inside. A wide alley down the middle of the barn was flanked by three stalls on either side. A big black horse raised his head from the bucket where he'd been searching for the last morsel of grain.

"Preacher!" Becca exclaimed.

Chapter 6
Indiana

A rush of memories swept through Becca's heart at her first sight of the tall, pitch-black horse standing in Merv's barn. She remembered the gangly newborn — the black colt with an unusual white marking on his chest. She'd only been 5 years old, but she remembered. She and the neighbor kids had played with him every day that summer. Later he'd gone away to Indiana — to be trained, her dad said — but he'd ended up on the race track. So Jonas brought him home, because Amish people couldn't own race horses. She'd been so thrilled to have Preacher back, and he'd become the family's buggy horse. How beautiful he was, and how he could run!

But that became a problem too, her father explained to her in the barn one evening. He was going to sell Preacher back to the racing stable. Because Preacher was too fast and too beautiful, and a man shouldn't have anything that would make him proud. How she'd cried as a big white horse trailer took him away one Saturday. But of course it was meant to be, the family believed, because the next day her father was made minister. And a minister shouldn't have a horse like Preacher.

She'd seen Preacher one more time. Her family was at a reunion in Indiana — she must have been about 8 — when Merv showed up and said Preacher was racing nearby. She could still feel the excitement of doing something forbidden. Her family really shouldn't go to the races, especially with her father being a minister. But they'd gone, and oh, what a feeling! The noise and tension of the crowd in the stands, the thrill of watching Preacher—her Preacher—win that race, pulling away from the rest of the pack! What a never-to-be-forgotten moment, and Preacher — what a never-to-be-forgotten horse!

Preacher nickered low and nuzzled Becca's outstretched hand. "Do you think … is it possible he remembers me?" she asked Merv.

"Sure, I think he could," Merv confirmed. "I also think he loves his grain, and there's always the hope that a hand will give him some."

Becca stroked the silky black neck as she took in the rest of the horse she hadn't seen for eight years. He looked heavier. Like Merv said, Preacher was no longer in trim muscular racing form — he'd become a lazy pasture horse. But he was older too, and who didn't add on a little weight with age?

"You're looking good, big guy," she said softly. "You remember me?"

"Your dad tells me you've become quite the horsewoman," Merv said, opening the door to Preacher's stall. "He says you ride your horse bareback like you grew up on him, and you drive the horse and buggy in town, no problem."

"I like horses," Becca answered. What was she supposed to say? That she'd rather be riding a horse than pedaling a sewing machine? That sometimes she felt she'd never settle down and be the Amish woman she was supposed to be? That sometimes she felt guilty, but she didn't know why she should feel guilty for who she was?

"Would you like to ride him?" Merv asked.

"Oh!" Becca couldn't believe her ears! Any trace of

tiredness slipped behind her sparkling dark eyes, and the beam across her face made Merv laugh out loud.

"I think I have my answer," he said, reaching for Preacher's halter and leading him out the door. "Bareback or with a saddle?"

Becca didn't know. She felt the most at home on a horse bareback. She could move with him, feel him between her legs, guide and cue him. But Preacher — he was so big! A racehorse! Fast! Could she control him? Hold him back if he started to run? Could she stay *on* him?

"I might be crazy, but I think I wanna try bareback," she said, noticing at the same time how incredibly tall he stood. She'd need a lift up, just to get on his back. No vaulting onto this one!

"I'll tie him and give you a leg up," Merv said, looping the lead rope into a sailor's knot in a sturdy ring on the wall. "Here you go!"

Becca sat on Preacher while Merv slipped a supple leather bridle over his ears. Nothing half-rate here, Becca noted. All of the tack was kept oiled and pliant. She loved the smell of Merv's barn — horses and leather. If she did nothing else in Indiana that weekend, this time at Merv's home with Preacher was enough.

"He's all yours," Merv said. "You can ride in the pasture here, or if you go west along the road, you'll come to a path into a field that's nice for riding too."

The pasture seemed too confined, Becca thought. Once she got the feel of him, she wanted to let him run. She opted for the road.

Preacher loved being out, she could tell. He obeyed her commands and kept himself at a walk, but it was the walk of a horse dying to break into a trot. When Becca felt comfortable with him and that he would obey, she let him go the next step. She hated the jarring trot, and soon allowed

Preacher into a very slow easy canter. That's when the smile started on her face — the smile that didn't leave for the next 30 minutes.

The smile spread after they turned onto the field road, and Becca let Preacher out another notch. They were beginning to fly now, the wind in her long curly hair, whistling past her ears. Preacher snorted and Becca felt the wetness come back at her. She laughed and gave him more rein. They were one, flying.

"Now I *really* need a shower," Becca said, sliding off of Preacher's wet broad back in front of Merv's barn. Her seat and legs were soaked with dirty brown horse sweat, and she still couldn't stop smiling. Merv was grinning too.

"I think you two are good for each other," he said, tying Preacher up again and reaching for a grooming brush. "I probably shouldn't be saying anything without talking to your parents first, but I had an idea while you were out riding." He paused and looked at Becca. "I was thinking, maybe this summer or next, you could come out here, stay at our place, and get a job in one of the restaurants or something. Give you a chance to meet some boys from another community, and we'd love to have you. Of course, Preacher would like having you around too."

The idea caught Becca completely off guard. Live someplace other than Kansas? The thought had never occurred to her. To be around Preacher all the time? That seemed too good to be true. Live with Merv and Ella? The woman could drive her nuts. But maybe she could get used to her. Would her parents even consider letting her do it?

"Wow, what an idea," she said. "I could ask them. I have no idea what they'd say."

"You'd have free room and board with us, and like I

said, the chance to meet guys other than those in Wellsford. Aren't you related to 'most everybody there anyway?"

Becca giggled. "Oh, maybe distantly, I don't know."

"Well, you think about it," Merv encouraged. "I can finish taking care of Preacher if you want to take a shower and catch a nap before your ride comes to pick you up again."

"That sounds really good," Becca admitted. Suddenly, she was very, very tired.

It seemed she'd just fallen asleep when Becca felt some-one gently shaking her shoulder and saying, "Becca! They're here to pick you up." She woke with a start to see Ella in her pink flowered dress. She wanted to tell her to go away, to let her sleep, but Ella's words reminded her she had to go. Al and the rest of the kids were waiting.

"I got your shorts washed, but they aren't quite dry," Ella said, holding the black jean shorts out to Becca. "I fig-ured they weren't much use to you as dirty as they were from riding."

"Thank-you. Thank-you so much!" Becca said, truly grateful. Bless her heart, Ella's motherliness was kinda nice to be around. She'd certainly be well taken care of if she lived with them.

"Merv had to leave to take some people shopping, but he told me to tell you to remember our offer. We'd love to have you come back, you know!"

"Yes, I know. Thank-you. I'll talk to my parents about it," Becca said. "I guess I'd better get going now — they're waiting on me."

"Oh, they'll wait, they'll wait. Can I send some cookies along with you?"

Before Becca could answer, she was holding a bag of

chocolate-chip cookies. She let herself out the door, Ella following along, and waved good-bye from the sidewalk. Then she turned toward the pickup.

"Hey, why'd you change back into the dress?" Myrene wanted to know as soon as Becca was in the topper. "What's wrong with my shorts?"

"There's nothing wrong with your shorts. In fact, they're great for riding bareback, but they got a little dirty," Becca answered, then quickly added, "So Ella washed them for me, but they aren't quite dry yet."

"Well, we're going to hang around the mall now, then go to a movie at 5:00," Myrene said. "By the time we head out to the party this evening, you'll be able to put them back on."

"Yeah," Becca agreed. The mall, a movie, a party. It sounded like quite an afternoon and evening ahead of them.

The mall wasn't a big deal, actually. She'd been to a mall a few times in Kansas, when her parents had hired a driver to take them to Vicksburg. The abundance of places to shop and spend money amazed her, and it was fun to look at things even though she couldn't imagine needing or wanting most of it.

The movie, now that was another experience. The group chose one that they explained to Becca would have a lot of excitement in it. Well, she guessed "excitement" was one way to describe what happened on that huge screen in front of her. It seemed that people were either driving their cars recklessly and having crashes, or they were yelling and shooting each other, or they were in bed with each other. And the sound! It seemed to surround them, to invade her eardrums, to pound into her very soul. Between the sounds of the throbbing music, the crashing car scenes, the shooting guns, and the sensuous love scenes, Becca felt she'd seen and heard it all. All and more than she wanted to. But maybe she was just being silly, she thought. It didn't seem to bother the rest of the kids. You probably just had to get used to it.

After the movie, the pickup full of teens cruised through the streets of the town, ending up at a pizza place for supper.

"So, Becca, you ready for your first Indiana party?" Al's handsome face could chew pizza and ask her a question at the same time, Becca noticed.

"Ready as I'll ever be," she answered, taking a sip of her Dr. Pepper. "Do you have any words of advice?"

"Oh, chust don't do what I do," Al said, and winked at some of the other guys. "It might be too much for a girl your age."

The guys laughed raucously, and a twinge of nervousness swept through Becca. She'd heard enough about some of the Amish parties to wonder what she was getting into. Of course she wasn't getting into anything she didn't want to, she reminded herself. She didn't have to do what the other kids were doing. She could still say no.

"I'll remember that, Al," she answered. "I will make a point of not doing what you're doing."

But it was Al who approached her later that evening as approximately forty young people sat around a deserted barn in a pasture. His pickup doors stood open, the music blaring into the muggy May evening stillness. Several coolers of sodas and beer sat stationed next to the barn, and kids were just hanging around, talking and drinking. A couple games of cards kept some of the youth occupied, and Al's laughter rang out over the group. He was telling a story again, and those around him could hardly get enough. The life of the party, that Al, Becca noted. Everybody sure liked him.

"Hot diggity! It's my favorite dancin' song!" Al suddenly

interrupted himself in the middle of his story. "I gotta find me a woman to dance this one with!" The words were no more out of his mouth than he was standing in front of Becca where she was leaning against the pickup with a group of other girls.

"And I choose this one!" Al said, taking Becca by the hand before she could protest. "Do you know the two-step? Here, let me show you." And again, before Becca could offer any resistance, his arm circled lightly around her, guiding her, his lithe, strong body moving to the beat. She could smell his cologne — she remembered it from the Star Bowl. And despite her surprise and initial embarrassment, she couldn't help but like what was happening. She had no trouble picking up the steps, and by the end of the song, she was loving every minute of it. The song ended, and the rest of the kids clapped.

"Mighty fine! Totally fine!" Al declared, looking down into her eyes. "Come 'ere!" he said, leading her toward one of the coolers.

"I want you to taste this," he said, picking a can of beer out of the ice. "You don't have to get drunk. Chust a little — it'll make the evening even more fun."

Becca hesitated. She didn't want to look like a prude in front of Al. Not after that awesome dance with him. She took the can. A sip. That's all. Maybe then he'd go away and she could discreetly pour the rest out.

She popped the top and took a swallow. She couldn't help but react to the unusual taste. Al laughed at her wrinkled up face. "You'll get used to it," he said, and sauntered back to the guys. "Now, where was I?" he asked.

Becca was just about to pour the can out when Myrene stopped her. "Hey, what are you doing? You pouring good beer out?" she questioned loudly — so loud Becca was afraid Al could hear her. "Just drink it, a little at a time,"

Myrene advised. "For Pete's sake, you don't have to worry about getting drunk on one can. It'll just loosen you up a little."

56

Chapter
6

Now Becca felt like everyone was watching her. Okay, so she'd sip on the beer all evening. Maybe she hadn't been able to say no to Al in the first place, but she still had control of herself and the situation.

By 11:00, the can was empty. She threw it away. By 11:30, Al noticed, and two-stepped her back to the cooler. The music playing on the radio wasn't even right for the two-step, but it didn't seem to matter. He gave her another can.

Chapter 7

Invitation

The trip back to Kansas on Sunday wasn't nearly as much fun as the one going to Indiana. Everyone was tired and no one felt very good. In fact, sleeping seemed to be the easiest way to pass the miles. In the back of the pickup, Becca worried about Al, who wasn't any better off than the rest, but who had to drive. Finally, at one of the rest stops, she got up her nerve and asked to trade places with one of the guys riding in front. He didn't really care because he could stretch out to sleep better in the back anyway. And Becca figured she could talk to Al to keep him awake.

"So, did you have fun this weekend?" Al started the conversation.

"Yeah, I did," Becca answered.

"Your first movie, your first beer. You're on your way now!"

Becca was quiet. What should she say? She'd held onto the second can of beer Al had given her, and managed to slip it back into the cooler. She didn't like the stuff, and she didn't like how the beer was affecting the other kids. They were doing and saying stupid things. By the end of the evening, she was one of the few who wasn't drunk. She didn't want to talk to Al about it. She didn't want to look like a party pooper. Even if she probably was.

"Do you go to Indiana often for parties and stuff?" she asked Al, hoping to steer the subject away from the night before.

"Oh, for sure if there's a wedding or a major party goin' on," he answered. "And sometimes, if I chust need to get away."

Chapter
7

As the miles and hours passed by, Becca found out that Al was really a nice guy. She'd suspected as much, but she'd never been sure how much was "show" with him and how much was sincere. Now, as they passed the time talking about his experiences during his four years of running around with the young folks, Becca knew she was seeing and hearing the real Al. Yes, he made her laugh with his stories of the shenanigans he'd done with the guys, but he also shared personal thoughts and feelings.

"When do you think you'll join church?" Becca asked at some point in the evening, as they cruised along the interstate. Everything was quiet in the topper behind them, and the other guy in the cab slept, slumped against the passenger door.

"Chust before I get married, I suppose," Al answered. "Don't see any point in choining any sooner."

"Have you ever thought you might not join?"

"Not really. Oh, I'll miss this baby," he said, patting the dashboard. "But when I'm ready to settle down with a wife and have a family, I'll be able to give it up."

"It just gets you in trouble anyway," Becca said wryly. "The pickup, I mean."

"Yeah, and I'm glad you see it that way," Al said, chuckling. "Some people think I'm a reckless, wild driver, but like you said, it's the pickup that does bad things."

Becca shoved Al's shoulder playfully. "You know what I meant."

"Hey, have you seen me being bad on this trip?" he

challenged. "I promised your dad I'd be good, and I have been. Haven't I?"

"Yes, I must admit, you have," Becca acknowledged. "At least, *most* of the time." Then, "Did you really promise my dad?"

Al's gray-green eyes left the road and looked at the girl next to him. "I'm still not sure why, but I did," he said, his voice uncharacteristically serious.

"Was it because he's a minister?"

"Yes, I think that had a lot to do with it," Al admitted. "It never hurts to stay on the good side of the preachers."

"Try being the daughter of one," she said, and then she didn't know why she'd said it. She didn't have any complaints about the way her father treated her. It's like it had been the thing to say, whether there was any truth to it or not. "Actually, it's not so bad," she added lamely.

"Would be for me," Al commented. "Especially the daughter part."

Her family, of course, was dying of curiosity about the weekend. Fortunately, Becca could tell them in good conscience that the best part was seeing and riding Preacher, and that the rest was okay but no big deal. And when she mentioned the idea of going to Indiana to live with Merv and Ella for a summer, she got the response she'd expected: "We'd have to think about that."

Apparently they were still thinking about it two weeks later, because Becca hadn't heard a word more about it. She'd made up her mind to ask, when, on a storm-brewing last day in May, the letter came from Pennsylvania.

Becca noticed, as she walked from the mailbox to the house, that the letter was from Amos Beiler, Sue Ann's brother-in-law. She wondered why he'd written — usually his wife, Sue Ann's sister, wrote the letters. Becca hurried into the house and handed the letter to Sue Ann.

Sue Ann read the letter silently, then just as silently folded it back into the envelope.

"Well, what's going on?" Becca asked, unable to wait any longer.

"Nothing," Sue Ann said, returning to the mending she was doing.

"Nothing?!" Becca was incredulous. "Amos never writes us! Why can't you tell me?"

"Because your father needs to read it first, that's why," Sue Ann answered, and Becca could tell something was bothering her. What could it be that she couldn't tell her?

She didn't find out that day. In the evening, the storm that had been building all day unleashed its spring fury. High winds and heavy rain thrashed through the Wellsford community, leaving behind swollen creeks, broken branches, and flooded fields of ripening wheat. The next morning, Jonas invited Becca to go along and assess any damage to their land. She jumped at the chance to be with her father outdoors.

They didn't have to walk far to find the first problem — their solar-powered electric fence that kept the cows in had been wiped out by trash and debris from the much-higher-than-normal creek. They would have to clear the junk out and put the fence back up again. Becca was glad to be bare-foot — she could just step in the creek and not worry about getting her shoes or boots wet. The cold mud squished between her toes, and the chilling water soaked Becca and her dress as high as her thighs. She shivered involuntarily and began pulling the wire out of the pile of branches. Dirty work, but she didn't really mind.

"As you know, we got a ltter from Amos yesterday," Jonas said, fishing one of the iron fence posts out of the mud. "He asked a very interesting question, and he wants an answer real soon." He picked up another muddy post. "One of the girls in his buggy rides business got sick and can't drive anymore. He's wondering if you want to go take her place for the rest of this summer."

Becca stopped, still holding the wire in the thigh-high water. Had she heard right? Amos wanted her to come to Pennsylvania to give buggy rides? To tourists? *Her?*

"He advertises his business to the tourists as 'only place you'll get a buggy ride given by an Amish girl,'" Jonas explained. "He's heard you're handy with horses, and is wondering if you want to come help out."

Would she? Could she?

"Would you let me go?" Becca asked when she finally found her voice.

"We've been talking about it," Jonas said. "Mom's not thrilled, as you might figure."

"Yeah," Becca said. "I thought the weekend to Indiana was bad. I can't imagine her letting me go to Pennsylvania for the summer."

"She has reason to worry," Jonas said, defending his wife. "A lot of bad things can happen."

"I know, I know."

"Anyway, I can't say we've come to a decision. But I thought I'd better ask you before we do. In case you don't want to do it, then your mom and I don't even have to talk about it," he said.

Becca's heart raced back to the hope she'd been holding that she could spend the summer with Preacher in Indiana. Then it jumped forward at the thought of going to a new community, to the opportunity to make money doing what she loved — being outside with horses. She couldn't do both. What if she'd go to Indiana and hate her job? Would it be worth it, just to be around Preacher? On the other hand, she might enjoy giving buggy rides, but what would the rest of her life be like in Pennsylvania?

Becca pulled the last of the wire buried in the debris and stepped out of the water. "Dad," she said, dripping on the creek bank. "I think I'd like to try this Pennsylvania thing."

"I kinda figured you'd say that."

The more she thought about going to Pennsylvania by herself to drive a tourist buggy, the more jittery Becca got. The only other time she could remember being so nervously scared and excited was when, as a seventh and eighth grader, she pitched her team to the league softball championship. The day of the game she couldn't eat a thing, and she couldn't think about anything else — the teachers knew she wouldn't be worth much in class that day. She could hardly wait to get out there and throw that ball, because she knew she could do it, but the stakes were high, and it drove her nerves wild. This Pennsylvania opportunity felt the same, with one additional big difference — it was faraway in a world of people she didn't know. And while she was dying for her parents to say yes, a small part of her knew she'd be relieved if they said no.

The answer, when it came, threw her heart into a cartwheel and sent her head reeling. Yes. Yes, because they knew and trusted Amos and Belinda. Yes, because they trusted her. Yes, because it would be excellent income for the summer — money that would go to her parents, as was the policy among Amish parents and their teenagers who worked outside the home. Yes.

That evening Jonas and Becca walked the quarter mile to their neighbors, the Jacobs family, whose phone they often used to call an "Amish taxi," make doctor appointments, or whatever other business they needed to do over the phone. They were going to call Amos and talk to him. One of the differences between the Wellsford, Kansas, Amish and those in Gary County, Pennsylvania, Becca had found out, was that many of the Gary Amish had phones somewhere on their property. It might be in the barn or in a small booth at the end of the lane. Often the phone was within hearing distance with the aid of a loud ringer; if not, they'd use voice mail to record the caller's message. Amos had told them to call as soon as they'd made a decision.

Becca watched as Jonas punched the phone number in quickly and without hesitation — including his own credit card number. They may not have a phone in their home, but he was certainly adept at using one. Then he waited, and waited, and waited.

"Gotta wait for them to hear it ringing, and then come from wherever they are," he explained to Becca, who nodded. Her stomach knotted. She wanted to pace the floor.

"Hello! Amos! It's Jonas!" she finally heard her father say into the phone.

Pause.

Becca was dying to hear the other side of the conversation, but she could only guess what Amos was saying, based on her father's responses.

"Yes, well, we've been talking about it. If you think you can take good care of her — she's only 16, you know — I guess we'd consider letting her go."

Pause.

"It's hard to let her go. Sue Ann and I — we wonder about this driving she's supposed to do. Is it a busy road? How safe are the horses?"

Pause.

"If the horse is traffic safe, she won't have any problems. But all of those tourists — how do they drive? Do they respect the horses and buggies?"

Pause.

"Yeah, I guess it's the same as here. Some do, some don't. It's just that you have so many more."

Pause.

"That's certainly part of the deal. If ever she doesn't like it or feels it's more than she can handle, she comes home."

Pause.

"Sure, you can talk to her."

Jonas handed the phone to Becca.

"Becca, we'd love to have you out here. Do you have any questions about this?" a soft friendly male voice asked.

"I don't even know what to ask," she said. "Um, how soon?"

"As soon as you can," Amos answered. "We'll be waiting for you."

Becca had so many questions, but she couldn't begin to ask them. Did she have to talk to the tourists? What was expected of her when she wasn't working? Who would she spend time with? Were her clothes okay? How were the Gary Amish different from those in Wellsford? What did the young folks do on the weekends? Would she be accepted by them? Did the tourists do and say stupid things, and how would she handle that?

"Becca? You still there?" Amos's voice asked, the sound of his voice bringing her back.

"Yes! I … I guess I'll just have to come out there and see what happens," she said. "Here's my dad again."

"Yeah, Amos," Jonas continued. "I guess now we have to find a way out there for her."

Pause.

"We'll ask around. I'd sure rather have her riding with someone than on a train or bus."

Pause.

"I'd heard that some of the Gary Amish had flown. Not here. No, she can't fly. We'll see what we can find."

Pause.

"Okay, we'll let you know.

Pause.

"All right. Good-bye."

Jonas and Becca thanked Cindy Jacobs for letting them use the phone, and then left to walk back.

"Dad," Becca asked in the deepening twilight of the early June evening, "have you been to Gary?"

"Once, as a teenager, for a wedding."

"What's it like?'

"A lot more people. Some things are different. Some the same."

"Will I like it?"

"I'm not sure. I guess you'll find out soon enough."

Chapter 8

Jo Pennsylvania

No one had plans to go to Pennsylvania in the near future — at least none of the "Amish drivers" in the Wellsford community. This was a busy time for the Amish farmers in Kansas — not a time for vacations or going to see relatives. Weddings in Pennsylvania happened in October and November, so that wasn't pulling people east. It wasn't a good time to catch a ride to Gary.

Becca was afraid her parents would cancel the whole thing, and again, she could almost see herself being relieved if they did. Another phone call to Amos provided what seemed to be a good solution: Amos was willing to pay not only Becca's train ticket to Gary, but he would also buy a round-trip ticket for Jonas or Sue Ann as well. "That way you can make sure she gets here safely, and you can see where she'll be living and working," he said. Jonas and Sue Ann just shook their heads in amazement. Amos must have a lot of money and be desperate for Becca to come work for him if he was willing to buy those tickets.

There wasn't any question as to who would be going. Jonas had to stay home to milk and do the farming. Lydianne was old enough to take care of Emma and make meals for the family, so Sue Ann would make the trip with Becca.

Cindy Jacobs, their neighbor and friend of the family, offered to take them all to the train depot in Vicksburg that

first Monday in June. They could have left on Sunday, but
Jonas wouldn't even consider it. Sunday was church day and
the Lord's day. You didn't spend it in a van, going to Vicksburg
to see your wife and daughter off on a train. No way.

So, at 3:00 a.m. on Monday morning, Cindy Jacobs and
the Bontrager family stood together outside the depot,
watching and listening for the arrival of the passenger train.
The city seemed strange at that time of night, without the
usual noise and congestion of people and traffic. Still, it was
so different from nighttime on the farm, where the only
sounds and light were those offered by nature. In Vicksburg,
lights artificially chased the darkness, and even at that hour,
cars cruised the streets. Becca wondered where those people
might be going. Why would anyone be up at that time of
night, driving the streets? Unless, of course, they were catch-
ing a train.

Chapter
8

A long, piercing whistle sounded in the distance.

"Listen!" exclaimed 10-year-old E.J., who was carrying
Emma, walking with her along the pavement. He stopped
and faced the sound. "Do you hear the train?" he asked.

Emma's eyes grew big in the fluorescent streetlight, and
she pointed in the direction of the sound. Another shrill
blast let them know the train was much closer, and by this
time, they could hear the sound of the engines. Emma
grabbed E.J.'s neck and hung on tight.

"It's okay. That's the train! Mommy and Becca are going
on that train!" he explained. Emma began to cry.

"You shouldn't have said that, E.J.," Lydianne chastised.
"Now she's going to be a mess for sure."

"Ah, she didn't understand that," E.J. retorted.

"She knows more than you think she does," Sue Ann
said, taking her daughter. "Come here, Emma, it'll be
okay," she said, holding Emma close and kissing her fore-
head. "You'll be all right, sweetheart."

"The question is, will you be all right," Lydianne commented above the noise of the approaching train. They'd been able to see the bright white light for awhile, but now the huge mass of thundering steel and iron was visible too.

"I'm not sure," Sue Ann said. "I don't like any of this, really. Leaving the rest of my family to get on a train to take my eldest daughter halfway across the country and then leave her there. No, I don't like any of this very much."

"Come on, Mom, we can have fun together on the train," Becca said, trying to sound encouraging. "You know how you love to watch people. I bet there'll be a lot of very interesting people to watch on the train."

With a huge WHOOSH of air and steel against steel, the train pulled to a stop not so far from where the Bontragers and Cindy waited. After a few minutes, several passengers stepped off the train. Becca moved toward the door, the rest of the family trailing behind.

The conductor smiled at the Amish girl. "You riding with us today, young lady?"

"Yeah, me and my mom," Becca said, indicating Sue Ann with a nod.

"Okay, ladies, then let's be boarding," the conductor said pleasantly. "We've got a schedule to keep, you know."

Sue Ann handed Emma to Jonas, gave him a quick kiss good-bye, and followed Becca onto the train. Becca stood at the front of the car they'd entered, uncertain what to do next.

"I think we just find seats wherever we want to," Sue Ann whispered. The car was dark, but Becca could see lumps in seats that must be sleeping bodies. Some were curled into one seat, others had taken advantage of both. She hoped it wouldn't be hard to find two seats together.

"You can go on to the next car if you can't find seats here," the conductor explained. "Anything that's open is yours for the taking."

They couldn't find two seats open in the first car, or the second, and Becca was getting scared they'd be split up. If only some of the people who were hogging two seats for sleeping would sit next to each other and just use one. Finally, at the end of the third car, they found an empty row. Becca quickly slid in, followed by Sue Ann. They looked at each other, and Sue Ann sighed audibly, "Well, here we are."

And there they were for the next 36 hours, except for the times when they went to the observation car to watch the countryside roll by outside the large windows, and for several hours off the train during its stop in Chicago. Sue Ann had brought food along for the trip, so the only thing they bought was drinks. Good thing, too, Becca thought, noticing the cost of a hamburger.

The mother and daughter passed the hours comfortably together, at times talking, at times in silence, Sue Ann busy with a cross-stitch project, Becca with her head in a book. And of course there were people to watch. Neither Sue Ann nor Becca had been around people of other cultures and ethnic groups for as long as they were on that train ride. Sure, they'd seen African-Americans, Hispanics, and Asians occasionally in Vicksburg, but this was different. Becca found herself intrigued with the different accents as they spoke English, or a different language entirely. She also found herself staring at the marked difference in physical appearance and dress. But then, she realized, she and Sue Ann must look and sound unusual too — dressed in their plain clothes and speaking their Pennsylvania Dutch dialect to each other.

Although the time passed fairly quickly, Becca was definitely ready to get off the train when it finally pulled into the station in Holling, Pennsylvania, at 3:00 p.m. the next day. Amos had said he'd be there to meet them, and he was.

A medium-sized man with a large salty-brown beard and faded brown eyes, he carried a few extra pounds around his waist. His smile was warm, his voice as soft as it had sounded on the phone.

"Welcome, Becca and Sue Ann," he said, as he extended his hand to one, then the other. "How was your trip?"

"It was okay," Sue Ann offered. "Long enough, though."

"I have a driver here, and we'll get you home as soon as we can," Amos said. "I'm sure you'll be anxious to clean up and have a good meal."

The drive from Holling to Amos and Belinda's home in Gary County clued Becca in to some of the initial differences between the Amish community she came from and the one she would be living in that summer. Like Indiana, there seemed to be so many people living close together! And because there were more hills and rivers, the roads weren't laid out in squares like in Kansas. There seemed to be a lot of cars on the country roads, but you could hardly call them country, Becca thought. The roads were all paved, and there just didn't seem to be much "country." At least not like she was used to.

They came upon a huge bus parked along the side of the road. A group of people from the bus was milling around a small wooden building.

"Tourists buying things from one of the Amish roadside stands," Amos said. "You'll find a lot of us Amish out here have businesses that cater to the tourists. It's the only way we can stay here and raise our families, because we've outgrown the land that's available, and it's very expensive, almost impossible, to buy land."

"You don't farm at all, do you?" Sue Ann asked.

"No, I just have the buggy rides, and of course Belinda sells quilts out of our house."

"It's amazing you can feed the family on that," Sue Ann commented.

"We do all right," Amos said modestly, and the van driver laughed.

"Don't let him fool you," the driver said. "Amos has the most successful buggy rides business in Gary County. He won't admit it, but he's a marketing genius. If there's one thing more fun than taking a buggy ride past Amish farms, it's having the buggy driven by an Amish girl."

Becca glanced at her mother. A strange look settled onto her face — a look Becca couldn't quite read. She knew, though, it wasn't a look of pleasure.

"Well, here we are," Amos said as the van slowed down to turn into a long lane. A medium-sized, obvious but not ostentatious sign at the road proclaimed "Beiler's Buggy Rides and Quilts." Becca could see that another tour bus was pulled up in the yard, between a large, two-story, very modern-looking house and a white barn. A horse stood at the hitching post, a buggy behind it.

"The people will be in the front room, the quilt store," Amos said. "We'll go in the back door. The girls will show you around."

Becca and Sue Ann shared the guest bed that night in the home of Amos and Belinda and their nine girls. They'd been up late visiting with the family, and now they lay, tired, in the darkness.

"When he said 'the girls will show you around,' he meant it!" Becca whispered, giggling.

"I knew they had nine girls, but it didn't really sink in until I saw them all," Sue Ann agreed.

"It's no wonder he uses girls for his buggy rides. That's all he's got!"

"Except for Barbara and Bonita, they're all too young yet," Sue Ann corrected.

"Yeah, but he'll have them coming up in age and helping for years!"

"I suppose. If they like that kind of thing," Sue Ann said, sounding weary.

"True. Some of them might help with the quilting."

"Good-night, Becca," Sue Ann said.

"Good-night, Mom."

Becca knew she should be tired, but she couldn't fall asleep. She was in Gary County! Amos had promised to show them around tomorrow, and then, late in the evening, they'd take Sue Ann to the train for the ride back to Kansas. And she'd be on her own. Alone in Gary County. Well, not alone — this family would be good to be a part of. But, much more than ever before, she'd be on her own. Driving a buggy full of tourists!

Her stomach did that before-game churn. She turned away from her sleeping mother and tried to tell herself everything would be okay.

Chapter 9

Gary County

Becca woke before daybreak in the strange bedroom, and for just a second she couldn't remember where she was. Oh yes, in Gary County, Pennsylvania. In the home of Amos and Belinda Beiler. She could hear birds singing through the open bedroom window, and the smell of cow manure wafted into the room. Strange, she thought, because the Beilers didn't have livestock.

She slipped out of the bed and walked to the window. Of course, the neighbors. Everyone lived so close together here, the sounds and smells of one farm could often be experienced by the family nearby. The farmer next door must have cleaned out his cow lot and spread it on his field the day before. Becca smiled to herself. Oh well, she wouldn't mind having some things that were familiar, things that reminded her of home — even if it was cow manure.

"Good morning!" Sue Ann's voice came from the bed Becca had vacated. "Did you sleep okay?"

"Great, once I fell asleep," Becca answered, turning toward her mom. "How about you?"

"I had dreams about being on a train and it wouldn't stop to let me off. We would go past the station over and over, and I could see you all standing out there, but the train wouldn't stop. I was crying, begging the conductor to let me off."

"That's terrible, Mom."

"It was! I even woke up one time, and I was crying. I sure thought you'd hear me."

"Nope, I didn't."

Sue Ann and Becca dressed in the early morning light that filtered into their bedroom, and made their way down the stairs to the kitchen. Belinda, a petite woman who appeared to be in her early 40s, stood at the kitchen counter, cracking eggs into a bowl. She smiled at Sue Ann and Becca.

"Good morning!" she greeted.

"Good morning!" they returned, and Sue Ann added, "Is there anything we can do to help?"

"Sure, if you want to, you can peel these potatoes," Belinda said, indicating a stack of spuds on the counter. "Becca, you can go see if the girls are getting up. Barbara and Bonita are supposed to be making sure everyone's out of bed and getting dressed."

Becca ran back up the stairs. She stood at the beginning of a long hallway, with four doors on either side. She and her mother had shared a room at the other end. She tiptoed down the hall, past the bathroom and the sewing room. The next door was closed — that was probably Amos and Belinda's room. The other four rooms were the girls' — and in only one of them was there any sign of activity. Barbara and Bonita were sitting on the sides of their bed, getting dressed.

Seventeen-year-old Barbara noticed Becca in the doorway. "Hi, Becca," she said. "You're up early! I figured you'd sleep in if you could."

"I guess it's habit," Becca answered. "I get up at 5:00 at home to help with the chores. You're lucky you don't have chores to do."

Barbara laughed lightly as she stood up. She was a very pretty girl, with reddish brown hair and long luscious eyelashes. "I may not have animals to take care of — just seven sisters. Eight, if you count her," she said, as she playfully tapped 15-year-old Bonita on the shoulder.

"As if you have to take care of me and the others!" Bonita retorted. "You've got that just a little bit wrong!" she said and turned to explain to Becca. "*I'm* the one who watches the girls while *she's* out there driving that buggy all day long!"

Becca giggled at the interplay between the sisters. Pretty much like her and Lydianne at home, she thought.

"I keep asking you if you want to trade places," Barbara said, standing in front of her sister, shaking her covering at her. "But when it comes right down to it, you don't want to." She put the covering on her head and tied the strings lightly under her chin. "'Cause you're chicken."

"I am not chicken," Bonita threw back. "I just don't want to spend my days with dumb tourists who ask the same questions all of the time. If that's my choice, then I'll stay home." She also put her covering on, and the two girls moved toward the door. Becca stepped aside and followed them into the next room, where two more girls still slept soundly.

Becca watched with interest as Barbara and Bonita woke up their seven sisters in their rooms. Some got out of bed with a smile; others grumbled their way to the bathroom. When they came to the youngest girls, ages one and three, Barbara and Bonita each took one and got her dressed. It didn't take long until everyone had trooped down the stairs and found their spots at the breakfast table.

After breakfast, Amos took Becca and Sue Ann out to the barn, where he kept the horses and buggies that were used in his business. The buggies were a little different from theirs in Kansas, Becca noticed. Gary County buggies had gray tops and sides instead of black, and the top corners were rounded, not square. The horses were all geldings and,

Amos explained, had been on the race track at some time in their lives. Most of the buggy horses in Gary County came from the track, he said.

The difference between these horses and Preacher, Becca thought to herself, was that these had been harness racers. They were Standardbreds — used to pulling a sulky. Preacher was a Thoroughbred and had been ridden on the track.

Amos kept more than twenty horses for the business. They all looked pretty much the same to Becca — basic bay horses with black manes and tails. Several of them had white socks.

"Will I be driving certain horses?" Becca wondered.

"We'll see how it works out. Barbara has her favorites. I guess you'll find out as you drive them whether you have a preference."

"Can we see where she'll be driving?" Sue Ann asked.

"Sure," Amos answered. "I was planning on showing you when we take a quick tour of the community today. In fact, Les should be here with his van pretty soon and we'll leave."

Les did arrive shortly. Amos asked four of his "middle girls" if they wanted to go along — Bethany, 11; Becky, 9; Betty, 8; and Bonnie, 6. That left Barbara at home to do rides, and Bonita and Brenda to help in the quilt store and take care of 3-year-old Berniece and year-old Bernadette.

Sue Ann, Becca, Amos, and the three girls got into Les's van and left the yard as a car turned from the road onto their lane. They passed the car, and Becca could see the faces of two older men in the front of the car and two women in the back seat. One of the men had his window rolled down, and he held what she had learned already was a video camera in his hand.

"People coming either for rides or the quilt store or both," Amos commented. "They're out early this morning."

"Do they film you and take pictures of you?" Sue Ann asked the question that had crossed Becca's mind too.

"Sometimes, but usually they're respectful," Amos said. "A lot of the tour guides and businesses tell them we don't want pictures taken, so they don't."

"Isn't it a pain, always being stared at and looked at funny?" Becca asked.

"I guess you get used to it. Tourism has become so much a part of Gary County, I guess we've learned how to deal with it and take advantage of it. Honestly, I don't know what we would be doing if we weren't in the buggy rides and quilts business."

"Not everyone can farm anymore," Sue Ann observed.

"No. There isn't enough land. It's already been divided and divided within families. Two things are happening — the Amish community is growing, and tourism has brought in more motels, restaurants, entertainment places, and shopping centers. There isn't enough land for all of that *and* for the Amish to continue to live off of it."

As they drove down the road that curved its way toward the nearby town of Blue Valley, Becca noticed that the people who were still farming were doing it exclusively with horses. Apparently the idea of using tractors hadn't split this community the way it had in Wellsford, and she commented to that effect.

"What you'll see here in Gary County isn't one split, but a number of different branches of Amish and Mennonites, each with a little bit different belief or tradition," Amos answered. "Where you have Old Order Amish in Kansas, some using tractors and some using horses, we have the 'Car Amish' that drive cars and the Old Order Mennonites that use horses and black buggies with square corners. Still, the largest group by far is the Old Order Amish."

"I see," Becca commented, noticing a beautiful new

brick home with a buggy beside the equally attractive shed. "Is that an Amish house? It's so pretty!"

Amos laughed. "I guess we don't have anything against a well-built home."

Becca was afraid she was in deep water, but her curiosity got the best of her. "But it's not ... plain."

Sue Ann gave Becca a look that Becca read loud and clear. She shouldn't have said that. Les was laughing heartily in the driver's seat.

"One of the things you'll see here, Becca, is that many of the Amish have money to spend, and they spend it on their homes," Les explained. "And you're absolutely right, 'plain' does not always seem like a good description."

Becca glanced at Amos in the passenger seat of the van. The last thing she'd wanted to do was embarrass him — the words had just come out. Was he mad at her?

She never really did find out. Les must have sensed the tension, because he quickly asked Becca and Sue Ann what new Amish homes looked like in Kansas. Becca let Sue Ann answer the question — she was too busy wondering about everything she was seeing.

And there was much to wonder about. How they tolerated the traffic, for example. It seemed like for every horse and buggy on the road, or for every team of horses working in the field, there was one car or bus of "English" watching them. Maybe that was an exaggeration, Becca thought, but not much of one. The roads crawled with cars of people looking, taking pictures, driving slowly, stopping unexpectedly.

Another thing she noticed was how many "English" businesses — motels, restaurants, gift shops — used the word Amish in their name. What made them "Amish," she wondered. She decided to ask Amos, hoping it was a safe question. His answer was, "Nothing. It's just a way to get people interested." It didn't seem to bother him. Becca was amazed.

And when Amos asked them where they wanted to stop for lunch, Becca couldn't help herself, and suggested a place she'd seen that advertised "Pennsylvania Dutch" cooking.

"Do you suppose they have *real live* Pennsylvania Dutch people making the food there?" she asked Les, beginning to feel more at home and ornery as the day went by. She could tell Les was getting a kick out of her, and it only egged her on. Amos was still doing his running commentary of the places they were passing and talking about different aspects of the community, and Becca absorbed it all. This was probably part of her education — she'd need to know this stuff to tell the tourists in her buggy.

Oh my goodness, she thought, and her stomach did a flip-flop. Within a few days, maybe even tomorrow, she'd be alone in a buggy with who knows who, telling them about the Gary County Amish.

They drove the thirty miles to Holling that evening, had a nice supper together, and then it was time to take Sue Ann to the train station. For some reason, Becca hadn't thought about how it would feel to say good-bye to her mother, knowing she wouldn't see her for several months. It hadn't been so bad when they left Kansas, because she was still with Sue Ann. But now, as they waited for the train to arrive, it hit Becca. She wouldn't see any of her family for several months. When her mother got on the train, Becca would be alone in a new world, a new family, and her first job ever. The hugeness of the newness hit her, and it almost felt like she'd had the air physically knocked out of her.

The train thundered into the depot and screamed to a stop. Becca told herself she wasn't going to cry, but when Sue Ann hugged her and tearfully told her to please be careful and she'd be praying for her every day, the lump in

Becca's throat got away from her. She didn't want Amos to think he'd paid all that money to bring an immature cry-baby to Gary County. But at that moment, she wasn't very sure herself.

Chapter
9

Chapter 10

Tourists

The next morning, right after breakfast, Becca followed Barbara and Amos to the barn and helped them hitch up two horses to the "tourist" buggies. They were expecting a busload mid-morning, and there might be other people stopping in before that. Becca would be riding along with Barbara this first day until she became comfortable with the route and what was expected of her as a driver.

"They'll probably ask you a lot of questions," Amos said across the back of the bay horse with the white socks. He was on one side, Becca on the other, as they fastened the harness and pulled the buggy shafts up and slipped them into the shaft tugs. "If you know the answers and want to talk, go ahead. If you don't, just say you're new here — you're from Kansas — and you don't know. Tell them to ask me when you get back, or Belinda in the quilt store."

"Do you talk to them?" Becca asked Barbara, who was working with a horse beside them.

"Depends."

"On what?"

"On the mood I'm in and what kind of people they are. Most of them are nice, but some are rude. Sometimes I pretend I hardly know English. That usually works."

Becca laughed, but Amos didn't. "You can do that as long as you aren't being rude yourself, Barbara," he admonished. "We want people to say good things about our rides. We want them to come back, and to tell others about our rides. It's putting bread on our table, you know."

"I know, Dad," Barbara said, sighing audibly. "I'm not stupid. When I don't know English, I am *very sweet* about it!"

Becca wanted to laugh again, but thought better of it. Barbara was going to be a fun teacher.

The bus arrived around 9:30 a.m., and one-by-one unloaded its sightseers. They looked to be about the age of her grandparents, Becca surmised. Many of the men, as well as the women, were wearing some type of shorts. Teenagers in shorts was one thing, Becca noted to herself, but this was interesting. Very interesting.

Three women, who looked for all the world like sisters, made their way toward the buggy where Barbara and Becca were standing.

"Would you like a ride?" Barbara asked politely.

"Yes! Oh! How delightful!" One of the women gushed.

"Will you girls be guiding the horse?" the second one asked.

"Yes, I'll be driving, and Becca will be along too," Barbara answered. "Here, watch your step, and we'll help you in."

Before long, Barbara and Becca were slowly making their way down the lane with the three women sandwiched together in the back seat of the buggy. The women kept up a steady stream of talking and giggling, of rehashing places they'd been and anticipating sights yet to see.

"Oh my! Aren't you frightened to go out on this busy road?" one of them asked as they turned from the lane onto the road.

"Socks does it all the time," Barbara said to reassure her passengers. "This horse has been on this road for years and years. He's very safe. We'll be okay."

Although she didn't want to say it, Becca felt the same misgivings the woman had expressed. She hoped she'd be accustomed to the steady stream of traffic when it came her turn to take over the reins. A safe horse was important, but he needed a good driver too.

"Are you girls sisters?" the one who asked most of the questions wanted to know.

Barbara looked at Becca, and Becca knew what she wanted. She was supposed to answer the question. Barbara wanted her to get used to talking to the people in the buggy.

"No, we aren't," Becca answered, turning to face the trio. "I'm just here for the summer. I'm from Kansas."

"Kansas!" the woman exclaimed. "Way out west! Are there A-mish in Kansas too?" She said the word Amish as if it rhymed with "famous."

"Why, yes, there are," Becca said. "There are Ah-mish in lots of different places besides here."

"Do tell!" the woman chattered. "And you drive horses and buggies too?"

"Yes," Becca said.

The conversation continued as cars whizzed past them. Even as she talked with the women, Becca noted how confidently Barbara drove Socks. They stayed on the busy highway for only a few minutes before turning onto a more winding, country road with Amish farms and fields interspersed along the way. This road wasn't without traffic, but it wasn't nearly as heavy.

"Go ahead and take the reins," Barbara whispered while the threesome oohed and ahhed among themselves at the neat flower and vegetable gardens on the Amish farms. "This is a good time to get the feel of it."

Becca's stomach jumped, and she hoped the horse wouldn't feel her nervousness through the reins. She could do this. She knew she could. The reins felt the same in her hands as did those of their buggy horse at home. She leaned forward, alert yet relaxed, and smiled at Barbara. Now she was beginning to feel at home.

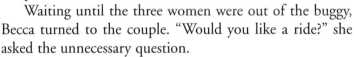

The minute Becca pulled Socks to a stop at the hitching post back at Beilers, a tall thin man and a trim, petite woman nearly ran over to the buggy. The man was wearing a white T-shirt and shorts that showed off his darkly tanned arms and legs, and the woman's skin was sun-browned, too, next to her perfectly matching sky blue shirt and shorts. He had a camera strap over his shoulder, and she carried an immaculate white purse with blue trim. Her shoes matched her purse, Becca noted.

Waiting until the three women were out of the buggy, Becca turned to the couple. "Would you like a ride?" she asked the unnecessary question.

"Yes, of course!" the woman answered, opening her purse. "How much is it?"

"Five dollars apiece, but you pay when we get back," Becca said. "In case you decide it's not worth it," she added with a broad winning smile. Amos had told her to say that. "The chances of somebody not paying are very, very small," he said. "But the chances of them tipping you if they liked the ride are quite good, so it's best to have them pay at the end." Amos was a smart businessman, no doubt about it.

The couple climbed aboard, and this time Becca took the reins while Barbara sat beside her in the front seat.

"Where are you all from?" Becca asked as Socks began his routine walk down the lane.

"Florida," the man said. "We live near Sunset, and there are a lot of Amish there."

"Many of them are either retired people, or young people who haven't settled down yet," his wife added. "We decided to come to Gary County to see another Amish community that is probably more typical than what we see in Sunset."

"I have a cousin in Sunset," Barbara said. "He's been there for a couple of years already, working on a construction crew."

"Really?" the woman asked. "We had an Amish crew build our house a year ago. What was their name, Kyle? Wasn't it Yoder something? Oh yes, I remember! The Yoder Boys, that's what they called themselves."

"The Yoder Boys!" Barbara exclaimed. "That's who Wayne is working for!"

"Well, I'll be," the man said, chuckling. "It's a small world, you know."

While Barbara and the couple carried on, Becca concentrated on driving Socks. When it came time to turn onto the busy highway, she felt a twinge of the jitters, but it left soon. Her route was all right turns so she didn't have to cross traffic. And the highway had a buggy lane, which helped immensely. Before long, she was slowing Socks down to make the turn onto the winding road.

Becca noticed a car stopped along the side of the road shortly after they made the turn. She looked at Barbara questioningly.

"Just go around it," Barbara said. "And if they take pictures, pretend you don't see them."

The words were barely out of her mouth when all four car doors opened and at least half a dozen people spilled out of the car. Most of them were children, Becca noticed. Children, and one woman. The kids were running around in the ditch as if they'd just been let out of prison, and the woman seemed to be trying desperately to get them under control. One of them was carrying something that looked like a huge plastic water gun.

Socks had been pacing at a steady speed and Becca immediately pulled him back to a walk. His ears pricked forward as he watched the activity ahead of him.

They were just even with the car when suddenly Socks jumped and lunged forward, breaking into a run. The woman in back screamed, and Becca instinctively pulled back on his reins and began talking to Socks.

"Whoa, Socks, whoa! It's okay! Whoa!"

Within seconds, Becca had Socks back in control, although he was still tossing his head and dancing away from the side of the road, as if expecting the horrible noise to happen again. The man was assuring his wife that everything would be okay.

"What was it?" Becca asked, glancing at Barbara beside her.

"I think the kid with the water gun hit him," Barbara answered.

"You're right! I saw it!" the man agreed. "He aimed it at the horse and hit his head. I can't believe how stupid some people are. If he didn't know better, his mother should have been keeping an eye on him."

"You did really good, Becca," Barbara said, complimenting her. "Dad will be proud of you when he hears what happened."

"I'm just glad Socks isn't a young or really spooky horse," Becca said, sighing. "We could have had a runaway for sure."

"Have you ever been in a buggy when the horse ran away with it?" the woman asked.

"I haven't," Becca answered. "Have you, Barbara?"

"No, and I'm glad today wasn't the first time," Barbara said.

"Oh, me too," the woman agreed.

When they got back to the Beilers, the couple thanked

the girls over and over for the ride, and for taking such good care of them.

"Here's the money," the woman said, handing Becca a $20 bill before stepping down from the buggy. "Keep the change as a tip—you deserve it today!"

The couple was barely out of earshot when Barbara nudged Becca and said, "Wow, I wish I'd have an almost-runaway so I could get $10 tips like that!"

Becca could tell Barbara was joking, but she also felt it was only fair to share the money. "Hey, I'll give you half of it," she said.

"I was just kidding," Barbara said as she studied the next couple approaching the buggy. "You don't suppose we could stage another one, do you?"

"Barbara!" Becca chided, and they both giggled.

That evening, as the large family and Becca sat around the table for supper, Barbara recounted the episode, much to everyone's interest. Amos said that had never happened before, and he couldn't believe it happened on Becca's first time out.

"I think you're ready to go on your own, don't you?" he asked.

"I think so," Becca agreed.

"And do you want Socks?"

"After what we've been through together, I think that'd be great," Becca said, and then added, "unless Barbara wants to drive him."

"Go ahead," Barbara said. "I've been wanting to talk to Dad about getting me a different horse to drive anyhow. Maybe now I'll have a good excuse," she said, and grinned at her father, who rolled his eyes and shook his head.

"You keep trying to spend any profit I might make on this business," he complained good-naturedly. "Next thing you'll want is a new buggy."

"Sounds good to me!" Barbara said.

Chapter 11
Ken

Becca had been at the Beilers for a week when, at midnight, the phone rang in the barn. She didn't hear it, but Amos or Belinda must have, because Belinda came into the bedroom and shook Becca awake. The walk outdoors to the barn in the muggy June air woke her up enough to wonder who might be calling and why. Hopefully nothing was wrong at home.

It was her parents, and no, nothing was wrong. They were just calling to see how things were going. Why'd they call so late? Oh, they forgot about the time difference — they were on their way home from a family get-together and saw that the Jacobs were still out in the yard, so they stopped to use their phone to call her — it was just 11:00 in Kansas and they figured the Beilers would still be up. But anyway, how was she doing?

Becca said everything was going fine. As she talked, she tried to decide if she should tell them about the water-gun incident. It might make them worry more, but it also might reassure them about Socks and her ability to drive him safely. She decided she'd better tell them, or else they'd probably hear it from Amos and then they would really think she was hiding something.

They took it well, and then her mother asked a question that threw Becca for a loop. Sue Ann wanted to know if she was homesick. If she was honest, Becca would have to say no. She'd been too busy and was having a great time. No, she wasn't homesick. That answer would probably hurt her mom's feelings, but it was the truth. So she said no, she wasn't, and Sue Ann was quiet on the extension phone while Jonas commented that it was probably too early and it would hit her after the newness wore off. Becca had to wonder if they wanted her to be homesick, as if that was some sort of reassurance of her love for them. Then Jonas said something she really didn't know how to handle. "Al asked when you're coming back," Jonas said. "I don't know why he wanted to know, but he asked."

Becca and her parents talked for a few more minutes, but it was the comment about Al that stuck in her mind as she walked to the dark house and got back into bed. Why would he want to know when she was returning? Was he just making polite conversation? Was there something coming up she should be home for? Did he, by any chance, *miss* her? No, it couldn't be that. Al was four years older and just being nice. He certainly couldn't have any feelings for her.

The Al question stayed with Becca into the next day, but she was soon preoccupied with all of the things to see and do and learn in Gary County. She found out that there were many different groups, called "gangs" of Amish kids. They had ice cream socials, played softball, and volleyball. Some partied and went to movies, and took weekend trips to the beaches in the summer and snow-skiing in the winter, but only the wilder ones. Some but not all of the guys wore English clothes, and all of the girls stayed in dresses. And most everyone made it to church on Sunday morning.

Church was very much the same as at home in Kansas. Some of the ministers were interesting to listen to, others struggled through their hour-long sermon. The songs were the same. And although she was usually very tired and had trouble staying awake through the services, Becca had to admit there was a certain sense of security in the sameness of everything. Being Amish tied her into a body of people whose traditions and beliefs bound them together, wherever they lived.

It wasn't just Amish people and tourists that Becca met in those first weeks in Gary County. The farm next door, for example, was owned by a Mennonite family, the Martins. In addition to their dairy farm, they ran a bed-and-breakfast in their home, and they were good friends with the Beilers. It wasn't unusual for one of the Martin boys to walk over and ask if the Beilers could give a buggy ride to someone staying at their bed-and-breakfast, and the Beilers would often mention "there's a great bed-and-breakfast next door" to their customers.

One evening toward the end of Becca's second week in Pennsylvania, as she was unhitching Socks after a long day on the road, one of the Martin boys came walking across the pasture from their farm. Becca knew the family had several sons, but she didn't know their names or ages. As this one drew closer, she could tell it was the oldest one.

"Hi," he said as he walked up. "You must be the girl from Kansas. My name's Ken."

"Hi," Becca said, smiling and taking him in with her steady, dark-eyed gaze. Average-looking guy, probably a few years older than she.

"We've got some people over there who are dying for a buggy ride," Ken said. "Any chance you'd be interested in giving them one?"

"Tonight yet?" Becca asked, stopping in her tracks. She was about to lead Socks away from the buggy.

"No, no, no. Tomorrow morning, after breakfast."

"Sure, that should work."

"Um, they usually come over and pick the people up at

our place. Is that okay with you?"

Becca grinned and answered, "Hey, whatever 'they' do I can do. What time?"

"9:00."

"I'll be there."

Ken started to leave, and then turned back. "So, do you like it here?"

"Yeah, I do," Becca said, pausing at the barn doorway. Socks pulled on the lead rope she was holding and reached for a clump of grass. "Anytime I can spend my day outside with horses, I'm happy."

"I can believe that," Ken said. "But you're not just with horses. You're with people all day too."

"True. Sometimes that's fun; sometimes it can be a pain."

"Don't I know. I work at the grocery store here in town during the summer, and you meet all kinds of people, that's for sure."

"Which store?"

"Blue Valley Grocery."

"Does your family own it?"

"Yeah. I've worked there during the summer ever since I was in junior high."

"Are you still in school?"

"Yeah, college."

"Where?"

Becca had just met Ken, but she knew an ornery grin when she saw one, and he had one on his face when he answered. "Kansas."

"Kansas? Where?"

"Oh, a small Mennonite college called Menno Simons, in the town of Marlow. Do you know where that is?"

"No, but then I haven't been around much," Becca acknowledged. "I'm just surprised you're going to college in Kansas."

Chapter
11

"Yep, come September I'll be back there," Ken said. "Well, I'd better get back and let you put the horse away and have some supper."

"Yeah, I need to get in," Becca agreed.

"See ya later," Ken said as he turned to walk away. "I'll be there at 9:00."

The next morning, at 9:00 sharp, Becca pulled into the Martin's yard with Socks and the buggy. She got out and waited for the customers to come out of the house. In a few minutes, a young attractive couple walked out, hand in hand, and Ken was with them.

"Jeanelle and Kurt, this is Becca Bontrager," he said, making introductions. "Becca, Jeanelle and Kurt are on their honeymoon, so give them an extra *lovely* ride this morning, will you?"

"I'll see what I can do," Becca said, and flashed her winningest smile. "Does that mean they want a fast ride or one that's nice and slow?"

Kurt burst out laughing, and Jeanelle giggled. Half-embarrassed, Becca glanced at Ken. The 16-year-old part of her was on the verge of giggling too, but the buggy-ride-operator part of her kept her face straight and innocent. Ken's expression seemed to be a mixture of surprise, shock, and amusement. She gave him a "I didn't mean anything" shrug, and the corners of his mouth turned up in a quiet, "yeah, right" kind of way.

"She's from Kansas," he said, giving the couple a large, obvious wink as they settled into the back seat of the buggy. "The Beilers have their buggy horses broke in pretty good, but they're still working on some of their drivers. Right, Becca?" The ornery grin — the one from the night before — came back.

"*Ich do nat fashtay,*" Becca answered in Pennsylvania Dutch. "Huh?"

Ken's grin split into a full-fledged guffaw, and he shook his head several times before answering. "Oh yes you do understand, you silly girl," he said. Then, turning toward the honeymooners again, he whispered loudly, "If you have any trouble with her, just let me know. I'll be happy to talk to her boss about sending her back to Kansas."

Becca threw a fake, squinty-eyed frown at Ken while Kurt and Janelle laughed behind her.

"Just you wait until I come into your store," she threatened. "When did you say you're working?"

The next day, Belinda asked Becca to go into town to pick up some things at Blue Valley Grocery, and Becca schemed for the two miles into town. Ken was beginning to feel like a big brother to her — someone she could tease. She'd get back at him for what he said the day before. Several ideas crossed and recrossed her mind before she settled on the one she liked the best. Yes, she'd get him good.

Tourists occupied the streets and sidewalks of Blue Valley, and Becca was glad she didn't have to come into town every day. Oh, she was getting used to being stared at, and she'd gotten to the point where she kind of enjoyed visiting with the people who took rides in her buggy. It was the steady stream of cars, buses, horses and buggies that still seemed so inconvenient and worrisome.

Becca turned Socks into the parking lot of Blue Valley Grocery and headed toward the hitching posts, only to see a row of cars parked in front of the space that should be reserved for horses. She turned Socks around and back to the street entrance. She'd have to find another place to tie up.

It seemed to take a long time before she could safely get Socks out onto the street again. She headed down the street for another place she knew had a hitching area, and the whole time, her mind was spinning. A new plan was taking shape.

Ten minutes later, Becca walked into Blue Valley Grocery and asked the clerk at the cash register if Ken Martin was there. The clerk said he was, and Becca asked if she could see him. Moments later, Ken came striding up to the cash register, his face breaking into a smile when he saw who was waiting for him. Becca wasn't smiling.

"I have a complaint," she said, and her voice meant business.

"Yes?"

"I came here to buy a lot of groceries, and what do I find when I go behind your store to tie up my horse? I find a row of cars blocking the hitching post!"

"I'm sorry," Ken apologized. "That shouldn't have happened."

"So how am I supposed to get my sacks and sacks of groceries way down the street to where I had to park?" she asked. She glanced at the woman at the cash register, who had a very puzzled, worried look on her face.

"I'm sure we could help you out with them," Ken said. Becca was having trouble keeping a straight face as she saw and heard Ken's distress.

"So, you're telling me that when I've purchased a month's supply of groceries for our family of twelve, you will personally help me carry the sacks out to my buggy?" Becca asked, allowing a slight smile to slip out.

Ken stood silently, studying Becca, and she saw the realization slowly growing in his eyes.

"It's none of my business, *ma'am*," he said, "but would you mind proving to me that you have enough cash on hand to buy all of these groceries for *your family of twelve?*"

Becca's dark eyes twinkled and danced and she let out the laugh that could hardly wait any longer. Ken joined her, and the clerk just stood there, bewildered.

Chapter 12

Funeral

Long days of giving rides soon turned into weeks, and the weeks flew by. Becca really liked her job, and had grown quite comfortable with her role as driver and tour guide. She was learning a lot, fast, about Gary County, and got a kick out of passing the information on to her riders. Her customers seemed to enjoy her too, and the tips proved it. Although her wages went home to her parents, she got to keep her tips, and the jar on her dresser was filling up with green bills.

One afternoon in the middle of July, Becca returned from giving a ride, and 9-year-old Becky came running out of the house, waving something in her hand. "Becca! Becca!" she hollered. "You got a letter! You got a letter!"

She hadn't received any other mail so far, and Becca wondered who had finally written her. Her parents had called once since the first phone call, but that was it. She took the letter from Becky's hand and noticed her family's return address in the corner.

Thankfully, no one was waiting for a ride, and Becca went into the house to get a glass of iced tea. Taking her tea and the letter, she found a shady spot under a tree in the yard and began to read her mother's handwriting.

Dear Becca,

I'm sorry I haven't written you sooner, but we are just so busy around here, and with you being gone, there's even more to do. I suppose you are busy too, because we haven't had any letters from you either.

First off, Daddy wants me to tell you that we had lots of rain on July 5 and 6. He says he kept track on the calendar, and that's 90 days since we had all that fog in April. He just wanted to make sure you knew that.

Becca smiled. Her silly father — he would remember that, and remind her of it. She continued reading as her mother filled her in on the activities of the family, community, and church happenings. She closed by saying they all missed her a lot, and hoped she was having a good time, and to Please Write!

Becca folded the letter and pulled another envelope out of the one the letter had been in. Lydianne's handwriting spelled out her name on the front. She tore the envelope open and read.

Dear Becca,

You are so lucky! You're up there having fun doing what you like to do while I'm stuck here doing all the usual stuff.

I'm sure Mom told you all the news from around here, but I had something else I thought you might like to know. I saw Al in the store the other day, and he asked about you. He asked if you're having a good time, and he wondered when you're coming back. I told him I thought you were having fun, and I didn't know when you'd be home. When are you coming back? I think he likes you.

I'll let you know if anything else happens.
Love, Lydianne

Becca took a long sip from her glass of tea and read Lydianne's short letter again. What was up with Al anyway? If he was so concerned about when she'd be home, why didn't he write and ask her?

"Somebody's coming from the Martins," 8-year-old Betty said that evening as the family sat around the supper table. She pointed through the window toward the neighboring farm. A man, silhouetted against the sun-setting sky, strolled through the pasture between the two properties.

"'Probably coming to ask about a buggy ride," Barbara commented. "And I bet it's Ken. I think he likes to come ask *Becca* about rides. If you know what I mean," she said, giggling and staring mischievously in Becca's direction.

Becca blushed at the insinuation. To be honest, she'd never thought of Ken as a potential boyfriend. He seemed much older, more educated, and well, he felt like a big brother, not a guy she'd want to date. And as far as appearance, Ken didn't match up with Al and some other guys she thought were really good-looking. He was a nice guy and they got along great, but anything more than friends had never crossed her mind.

A knock on the door let them know that whoever it was had arrived. Barbara stood up and went to the door, returning shortly with Ken. "Ken's wondering about a buggy ride tomorrow morning. Becca, what do you think?"

Becca wanted to throw Barbara a dirty look. Instead, she gazed calmly at Ken and replied, "I think I could make that work."

"Good," Ken said. "About 9:00?"

"Sure."

"Sit down and have some dessert with us," Amos said. "I think the girls made some pie today. Am I right?"

Bonita nodded, and Ken didn't have to be asked twice.
Ken stayed and visited with Amos while the girls did
the dishes, and when Becca went outside to take the meal's
scraps to the cats, she heard footsteps behind her. "Becca,"
Ken's voice called in the darkness.

"Yeah?"

"I was wanting to talk to you a little bit."

"Okay," Becca said, stooping down to dump the food
into the cats' bowl.

"I was wondering —"

The shrill sound of a siren split the peaceful evening air
and stopped Ken mid-sentence. It seemed to be coming
from Blue Valley. Becca wondered what had happened, but
she was also curious about what Ken wanted. The siren
seemed to be growing closer.

"I wonder what that's all about," Ken said.

"I think it's coming this way," Becca observed.

Before long, they could see the rotating red and yellow
lights on top of the vehicle as it screamed its way on the
road toward the Beiler farm. Passing the farm, it slowed
down and turned into the next lane.

"Something's wrong at home!" Ken cried out, and left
on a run. Becca ran toward the house and met the whole
Beiler family on their way out. A police car next door could
only mean bad news.

The Beilers and Becca walked through the pasture
toward the Martin farm, pulled by the traumatic magnet-
ism of the throbbing lights. They arrived at the edge of the
yard just in time to see the car tear down the driveway and
out the lane. It looked like Ken, his mother, and brothers
were all in the police cruiser.

Early the next morning, the phone in the Beiler barn
rang, and Amos sprinted to get it. He walked back to the
house, his head down, to tell the others the news. Two

101

Chapter
12

Amish teenage boys had hit Ken's father's car head-on in a one-lane covered bridge. Ken's father died at the hospital. The boys weren't seriously injured. They'd been drinking.

For the first time that summer, Becca missed her family. She wanted to go home. She wanted to get away from the deep shock and sorrow permeating the community. Everyone knew Leonard Martin because he owned the grocery store in Blue Valley, and everyone thought the world of him. For him to lose his life because two Amish boys were drinking and driving was completely unfair. Unfair and devastating.

Becca was angry too. Angry at the boys whose selfish actions and lack of responsibility had snuffed out a life. Angry at the alcohol that dominated weekends for many Amish teenagers from Kansas to Indiana to Pennsylvania. Why? Why did they have to drink in order to have what they called a good time? WHY?

Leonard Martin's funeral was held in the large brick Valley View Mennonite Church. Becca had never been inside a church building before she filed in with the Beiler family that Saturday morning in mid-July. The hot muggy air hung heavy among the several hundred people crowded into the church pews. Extra chairs were set up in the basement. The people kept coming.

The minister began the service by saying the family wished to thank everyone for their prayers, food, and expressions of concern. He then went on to say the family had planned the service as a time of praise and thanksgiving to God for Leonard's life, and although there was much sadness among them all today, it was the family's hope and prayer that Leonard's funeral, like his life, would be a witness to his faith in God.

Becca listened in amazement. What kind of a funeral was this?

For the next hour, she absorbed the words and music of people seeking, in the midst of their despair, to celebrate the life of a man of God. She absorbed but she didn't understand. The Amish, who were certainly also people of God, wouldn't celebrate a person's life at his or her funeral. It wouldn't be respectful. Funerals were a time for somberness and for those in attendance to evaluate whether or not they were right with God. Funerals were for soul-searching and submitting to the ultimate will of God, even if that meant the taking of a man in his prime of life.

But this was so different. The language was not of a man "taken" so early, but of a man who had passed from one life to another. Rather than hours of sermons from several ministers, there was a short message on the abundant life Leonard had enjoyed on the earth, and what he was enjoying now in the presence of God. There was a sincere prayer for the boys who'd hit him, asking God to work in their hearts and minds, and to forgive them. Then family and friends shared recollections of Leonard, speaking of what an impact he'd had on their lives, of special memories and incidents they remembered.

Becca's upbringing told her this kind of talk about a person didn't fit in with *Gelassenheit* — the underlying philosophy of Amish culture. *Gelassenheit* included the concept of humility, and humility didn't seem to fit in with what she was seeing and hearing. Yet, despite those misgivings, Becca found herself intrigued with what was happening. The sharing about Leonard made her wish she'd known him, and it didn't make him seem like a proud person at all. She looked at the rest of the Beilers and wondered if they were as confused as she was. She couldn't read anything in their somber faces.

Ken was standing at the microphone. Becca couldn't

imagine herself talking in front of the church at her father's funeral, but there he stood, his voice strong and clear.

"Not too long ago, my father called me over to his desk at the store," Ken began. "He showed me a quote he'd written on a card and slipped under the glass on his desk. The words were from Winston Churchill, and this is what it said: *We make a living by what we get, but we make a life by what we give.* 'Ken,' he told me, 'whatever you do in life, I want you to remember this quote. I want you to remember that it is more important to be successful at life than to be successful at making a living.' Then he asked me if I knew the difference, and I told him I did.

"Of course I never dreamed that day that my father wouldn't be with us much longer," Ken paused, and for the first time his voice broke. Becca's eyes misted, and she swallowed hard. How could Ken do this?

"I sat at Dad's desk yesterday and read that quote again. And I noticed that next to it he'd written, 'I have come that you might have life, and have it more abundantly. — Jesus.'"

Ken stopped again, then continued. "Dad lived and gave of himself and his material possessions abundantly. I pray that we will all learn from his example."

Ken returned to his seat among the family. Becca wiped her eyes with her handkerchief, and noticed Belinda, Barbara, and Bonita doing the same. Amos sat staring straight ahead.

The congregation was asked to stand and sing a certain number in the hymnbook. Becca opened the book to a song titled "Praise God from Whom." The singing began, and Becca stood mesmerized. The music began to swell around her in harmony — loud, strong, full-bodied, rising, enveloping. The words were of praise to God, and then the words changed to "hallelujah" over and over again, alternating between men's and women's voices, high and low. The melody built to a crescendo of "hallelujah, amen" and as the last note hung in the air, Becca felt a chill travel through her being and saw goose-bumps on her arms. She wiped her eyes again, but this time found herself smiling.

Chapter
12

Chapter 13

Warning

The evening of Leonard Martin's funeral, Becca wrote home. She told her parents about the accident, and how shocked the community was. She told them she'd been in a church building and how strange that felt. Growing up in the Amish tradition where homes were both a place to live their daily lives and have worship services, the thought that people needed to go to a special building to worship God was strange and uncomfortable. A church building was worldly, without a doubt. Why pour all of that money into a separate building, she'd heard her father explain, when they could hold their services in their homes? Having a separate building was just a step closer to the world. Next would come Sunday school classes, then dropping the German language. Before long, the people would be driving cars and using electricity, wearing worldly clothes, and sending their children to high school. Becca remembered her father saying that kind of progressive thinking is what led to so many different groups in Pennsylvania. Now she was seeing what he'd been talking about.

The part Becca couldn't understand was her own reaction to the funeral service in the church building. She didn't write any of those feelings to her parents, but she did to Lydianne. She told her how unusual the service was, and how the people had celebrated Leonard's life even as they mourned his death. *And the song at the end was so beautiful, I was just smiling and smiling,* she wrote Lydianne. *Can you imagine smiling at a funeral?*

Becca went on to tell Lydianne about Ken, and how she'd pulled a good one on him at the grocery store.

> *The night of the accident, he was here asking about a buggy ride, and he was going to ask me something else when we heard the sirens. I don't know what he wanted, but I suppose if it was important, he'll ask again. He's a nice guy — kinda like a big brother.*
>
> *By the way, how's Al? Tell him if he's so curious about how I'm doing, he can write and ask me himself.*

Becca put Lydianne's letter in a separate envelope before stuffing it into another envelope with the one to her parents. Maybe she'd actually get a letter back from Al! Now that would be fun.

Becca mailed the letter the next day. She didn't know how long it would take to get to Kansas, or if and when Lydianne would give the message to Al. And if she did, she didn't know if he'd write back. Yet, despite those uncertainties, she found herself wondering when the mail came every day if there might be a letter for her.

Two weeks later, 6-year-old Bonnie met Becca when she returned from giving a ride. She carried an envelope in her hand, and Becca's heart jumped.

"You got a letter," Bonnie said, holding the envelope up to Becca. "Who's it from?"

Becca recognized her mother's fine, perfect handwriting immediately, and answered, "Oh, it's from my parents." She slid her finger under the flap.

Dear Becca,

We were sorry to hear about the death of your neighbor. That is so sad, especially since it happened because some boys were drinking and driving. I think you know now why I'm concerned about you and the young folks you are with. Do you know those boys? What's happening to them now? And what about the family next door? How will they get along without Leonard?

Becca continued reading her mother's questions about life in Pennsylvania and her report on what had been happening in their lives. Then, to her surprise, Becca read:

I'm going to call it quits now and turn this over to your dad. He wanted to write you a few words too.

Becca rushed ahead to her father's square printed words.

I'm sure Mom has filled you in on all of the latest news around here, whatever that is, so I don't have to do that. Don't kid yourself — I wouldn't anyway. I don't like to write that much. But I did want to write you about something that's been bothering me ever since we got your letter.

Lydianne told us you'd written her about Leonard's funeral, and that one of the things you said was you'd been smiling at the funeral because one of the songs was so beautiful.

The little snip, Becca thought. I can't trust that girl at all.

I have mixed feelings about this, Becca. Enjoying good music is okay, and I wouldn't be saying anything about it except that there's a part of me that's a little bit scared. I'm scared where this might lead you.

I know, because I've been there. When I was your age, I visited a non-Amish group of teenagers — a church youth group. Some of the things about their faith impressed me, and I asked a lot of questions. But I also realized that I was born and bred Amish, and that is what I am meant to be. The jump to the world is far too big for those of us who are raised Amish, and I doubt that the people who do it are truly at peace with themselves.

Where is this coming from? Becca wondered. I go to the neighbor's funeral, I make the mistake of telling my tattletale sister that I smiled because a song was pretty, and my dad has me leaving the church!

She read on, and almost laughed. Yes, her father knew her well.

I know what you're thinking. You're thinking I'm jumping to conclusions. You may be right. But having been there, and now seeing you experience some of these things for the first time, I want to let you know that I'm concerned about the choices you make that will affect the rest of your life.

Enough said.

Love, Dad

Becca folded the letter up and put it back in the envelope. She'd have to read that part again, later, when she had time to think about it. She was used to her mother warning her about this and that, but this stuff from her father surprised her.

❖ ❖ ❖

The next evening, Ken came walking slowly over to the Beilers. Becca and Barbara were bringing the laundry in from the tall line strung between the house and the barn. Ken had barely greeted them before Barbara announced, with a very silly smile, that she'd be taking her armload of clothes inside now. The insinuation wasn't meant to pass over Ken, and it didn't. He smiled slightly at Becca, who was also holding an armful of clean clothes. Despite his smile, Becca saw sadness still lingering in Ken's eyes and across his face. Yes, he'd been strong at the funeral two weeks ago, but without a doubt, Ken was missing his father, and it showed. Becca hadn't talked to him since his father's death, and she wasn't sure what to say.

"Hi, Ken," she answered his greeting, then felt stuck. Talking about buggy rides seemed too trivial. Talking about death seemed so heavy.

"I thought I'd come over and let you know what I started to ask you the night of the accident," Ken said. Becca missed the lightness she was used to in his voice.

"I have wondered about that," Becca admitted.

"Well, it's kinda after the fact now anyway," Ken said. "Our youth group was planning an evening of volleyball, softball and other games that coming Sunday evening, and I was going to see if you wanted to go."

"Oh, that would have been fun," Becca answered.

"Yeah," Ken said, and then seemed at a loss for words himself. His head was down, watching as the toe of his shoe pushed a small piece of rock around on the ground. Finally, without looking up, he said, "Would you like to go for a walk? I ... I just need somebody to talk to for awhile."

"Sure," Becca answered. "I'll just take this laundry in and I'll be right out."

Moments later, the two were walking slowly down the lane in the quiet twilight. The windless evening hung softly around them, bringing the sounds and smells of the neighbor's cows their way, along with the buzz of cicadas in the trees and the trill of a mockingbird in the big elm tree at the end of the lane. The mockingbird reminded Becca of the one that often sang in a cottonwood tree back home, and she felt a pang of homesickness. She wondered what her family was doing tonight. If only she could pick up the phone and call them.

Chapter
13

"Had you ever been in a church before? Before the funeral?" Ken asked, looking straight at Becca with his medium blue eyes.

"No, never."

"How did it feel?"

"Strange."

"Being in the church building, or the funeral itself?"

"Both. But I got used to it. It was really okay."

Neither one said anything for awhile as they continued to walk.

"You were really brave to be able to get up and talk like you did," Becca finally ventured.

"Sometimes I think I was stronger then than I am now," Ken said, and Becca could tell that he couldn't look at her as the words emptied out of his soul. "I'm the oldest boy. The others — even Mom — are looking to me to help make decisions. Like about the store, and the farm. Even though he had people working for him, Dad's the one that held everything together."

"I didn't know him, but he sure sounded like a neat man, from what everybody said at the funeral."

"He was, Becca, he was." Ken said, his voice breaking. Becca knew what she would see if she looked at Ken then, and she dropped her eyes quickly. She couldn't invade his space, witness his hurt. She just couldn't.

They'd reached the end of the lane, and without a word,

turned toward the Martin's farm. Ken reached into his back pocket and pulled out a blue bandana. He blew his nose, then stuffed the handkerchief back.

"It feels like I've used a handkerchief more this summer than all the winters of my life put together," he said.

"I can't imagine how it must feel."

"It feels like when you get the wind knocked out of you. Something tells you that you're going to be okay, that the air will come back. But at the moment, you can't quite believe it. You think you're going to die."

"What *will* happen with the store and the farm?" Becca decided to ask.

"We're still talking about it. Mom says that after I get out of college, I should come back and take over the store. The farm — I'm not sure. My brothers might be able to handle it, with some hired help."

"Do you want to take over the store?"

"It sounds like a big responsibility. But as far as the kind of work it is, yeah, I could see doing that."

They had reached the lane turning into the Martin farm, and it was getting dark.

"Shall we walk back to Beilers through the pasture?" Ken asked.

"Sure."

"So, what do *you* want to be when you grow up?" he asked. A hint of lightness had returned to his voice, and Becca was so happy to hear it.

"A little Amish mother of twelve that comes into your store and bothers you," she said, giggling.

"That's fine — I already have practice at that," Ken responded and laughed in return.

"I don't want a dozen kids though," Becca said more seriously. "I don't like housework, and a dozen kids sounds like an awful lot of cooking, cleaning, and laundry."

"I bet you'd rather spend your life giving buggy rides," Ken said, and Becca could hear the smile in his voice in the darkness.

"Not in the winter," Becca was quick to point out. "Besides, I'd have to be an old maid who couldn't find anything else to do before that would happen."

"Why? Because all Amish girls get married and stay home and have children?" Ken guessed.

"Exactly."

"And I don't suppose you'd ever consider not being Amish."

Becca had heard those words before. She'd heard herself ask Al that question. But she'd never turned it on herself. Never.

"Not really," she answered Ken. "I can't imagine it, and besides, my parents would have a fit. I already got a letter from my dad, warning me against ever leaving the church." The words were out of her mouth before she knew it. Oh no, she thought, now she'd have to tell Ken why her dad was upset. All because of the music at his father's funeral. No, no, she couldn't tell him that.

"Why's your dad warning you about something you can't imagine doing?" The question came just as Becca had expected.

"It's a long story," she hedged. "Too long for tonight. Maybe I'll explain some other time."

They'd reached the Beiler yard, and everything was quite dark outside now. The glow of propane lights filtered through the curtained windows of the house. Becca knew the family would be getting ready to go to bed.

"Okay, but I'm gonna hold you to that," Ken said. "You've got me curious now."

"Yeah, well, curiosity killed the cat, you know," the words were once again out of Becca's mouth before she realized their potential venom. Any other time, it would have been a harmless cliche. But to Ken, for whom death was such a recent wound ...

"And I am not a cat, so I'm safe," he retorted with a chuckle. Becca almost heaved an audible sigh of relief.

Chapter 14

Questions

Something happened between Becca and Ken the evening of their walk together, and from then on, they spent a lot of time together. Becca had never had a boy who was such a good friend. In fact, the more she thought about it, she realized she'd maybe never had a friend quite like Ken. Except for Lydianne, who didn't count, because she was her sister.

But that was the interesting thing. Becca found herself sharing things with Ken that she would only tell her sister, if that. She told him about Al, and how she wondered if Al might be liking her, because he kept asking about her. She told Ken about the party in Indiana, and how much fun it had been to dance with Al. She told him the drinking among the Amish teens had sort of bothered her then, and now, after the death of Ken's father, it really made her mad.

Becca knew the reason she could talk so freely with Ken was because he was such a good listener, and because he was willing to share personal things with her too. He talked about having one steady girlfriend for about six months in high school, but not dating anyone for any amount of time since then. He said there were some girls at college he wouldn't mind taking out, but for some reason just hadn't. He said that he knew he was just an average-looking guy, and most girls wouldn't be dying to go out with him.

Becca assured Ken that he was so nice, surely girls would want to go out with him. Yet even as she said it, her conscience twinged. *She* didn't particularly see Ken as someone she'd fall all over herself to date. He wasn't good-looking, sexy-smelling, and flirtatious like Al. She couldn't imagine her heart thumping with Ken's arm around her waist like it had when Al taught her to dance. Ken was probably right — girls wouldn't be standing in line to date him.

Another thing they talked about more than Becca would have ever imagined was religion. Religion, and God, and Christianity. The topic first came up when Becca finally told Ken why her father had been warning her against leaving the church, and how much she had enjoyed the music at Leonard's funeral. Ken asked Becca a lot of questions about what she had been taught, and what she believed. And then he told her what he'd been taught, and what he'd discovered for himself, and what he believed about God.

Their discussions left Becca very confused. For one thing, she'd never really thought about any of that stuff before. She went to church because that's what the family did. She knew her father had to be a very spiritual person because he was a minister, and she knew her mother talked about praying for her and the other kids. But as far as she was concerned, getting serious about God was something a person did when they were going to join the church. And you didn't join the church until you were done running around and had found someone to marry. That's when you started to take religion seriously. That's when you joined the instruction class and found out what it meant to live by the *Ordnung,* the rules and standards of behavior that Amish were expected to follow.

But for Ken it was very different. Becca expected that. He wasn't Amish, so he wouldn't understand. What she didn't expect was her intrigue with what he said. She didn't expect to be interested in talking about God.

But she was. And for every question Ken asked her about her upbringing, she had one for him about God. Sometimes neither of them knew the answer, and sometimes they played a game where they'd make up the answer and try to fool each other. They had a lot of fun with it, and they learned a lot from each other too. And Becca found herself wondering what she'd do when she went back home and wouldn't have Ken to talk to anymore.

Chapter
14

One day near the end of August, Becca was sitting in the quilt store with Barbara and Bonita, talking and waiting for customers. They were discussing which couples would surely be getting married that fall — even though they hadn't been officially announced yet, the girls could make some pretty accurate guesses based on who had recently joined church or was in the process.

"You're going to stay for the weddings, aren't you?" Bonita asked Becca as she stitched a pillow case together. The girls contributed their own handiwork to the quilt store, and it was a nice source of cash for them.

"I don't know. I'd always thought I'd go home at the end of the summer, but Amos keeps saying he needs me to stay. I guess I'm here until he doesn't need me anymore or my parents say it's time to come home."

"You've gotta be here for the weddings," Barbara pitched in. "You talk about fun — now those are fun!"

"I can imagine!" Becca said, giggling.

A car pulled into the lane, and the girls watched as a middle-aged couple got out. Becca couldn't believe her eyes, but she was certain she recognized them. She hurried out the door.

"Merv! Ella! What in the world brings you here?" she exclaimed, greeting the beaming couple as they walked toward her.

"Well, we had to come see this horsewoman on the job," Merv said, his grin broadening even more.

"How are you? How are you?" Ella bubbled, and reached out to give Becca a hug.

"I'm just great!" Becca said into the little white prayer covering on the back of Ella's head. "I can't believe you came to see me."

"Well, you and a few others too," Merv said, laughing. "So, do we get a ride? Your dad tells me you've been a busy girl giving rides this summer!"

"I have, that's for sure. Let's go!" Becca said, leading them to the hitching post where Socks was tied up with the buggy behind him. "This is Socks," she said, mostly for the benefit of Merv. "He's okay, but he's not Preacher. How is he anyway?"

"He's fine, just needs somebody like you out there riding or driving him," Merv said, helping Ella into the buggy, then sitting down in the back seat next to her. "He's fat and lazy, just like he was when you saw him this spring."

Becca gave a gentle tug to Socks' reins and they left at a trot down the lane. Becca knew Merv was watching her, and she knew she looked confident driving Socks. Well, she should. She'd been doing this for several months now. A smile slipped out of her eyes and lips.

"So, are you coming back here next summer, or do we get a chance at you?" Merv asked, leaning forward in the seat. "You know, it was our idea you go someplace else for the summer, and you end up in Pennsylvania instead of Indiana. It's not fair, you know."

Becca recognized Merv's tone of voice as light and teasing, but she also knew he meant every word he said.

"I guess I haven't thought that far," she said.

"You're really good with horses, Becca," Merv said. "I still think you could get a job at Springdale Stables. In fact," he paused as if contemplating whether or not to continue. "In fact, I think you could make a career out of being with horses if you wanted to."

Becca laughed out loud, then turned her bright dark eyes on Merv behind her.

"Show me an Amish girl with a career in horses, and I'll show you a guy having the babies."

Merv and Ella both exploded into laughter, and Becca thought Ella would never stop. For pity sakes, it hadn't been that funny.

"You're probably right," Merv agreed after he recuperated. "You didn't hear me say this, and you won't ever tell your father that I did, but I suppose that's where you'd have to make a choice."

Choice. The same word her father had used.

"But you're too young for that," Merv said, reassuringly. "You're just 16, right? You've got time. Try it for a few summers — working with horses here or in Indiana. Maybe that'll help you decide."

"Or maybe some young Amish guy will sweep you off your feet and you'll forget all about horses, even if he doesn't have the babies," Ella said, bursting into another round of giggles.

"Yeah, well, we'll see," Becca said. "I've got an idea," she said, feeling the need to change the subject. "How about if we go into town and get some cold drinks at Blue Valley Grocery? I know somebody there who'd like to meet you— I've told him all about Preacher and how you helped him become a race horse."

"Him? You're taking us to meet a him?" Ella asked, and began tittering again.

Becca decided to ignore her. She wouldn't understand anyway.

❖ ❖ ❖

Later, much later that evening, Becca lay in bed in the hot bedroom at Beilers. At least in Kansas there was often a breeze to blow the heat around. That wasn't the case as often in Pennsylvania, and tonight was no exception.

But it wasn't just the heat keeping her awake. Her mind wouldn't go to sleep. It kept replaying the evening's conversations over and over, re-running the words and feelings.

Upon meeting Ken at Blue Valley Grocery, Merv and Ella had insisted on taking him and Becca out for supper. Fine. Neither Becca nor Ken would turn down a good meal.

The "Pennsylvania Dutch" cooking at the restaurant overlooking the picturesque countryside was great. Ken and the Smuckers hit it off immediately — all three were Mennonites who quickly discovered by playing "the Mennonite game" that they knew some of the same people. Becca almost felt left out for awhile, and then the conversation changed, and she very quickly wished she *would* be left out again. Because she was the focus of the discussion.

Merv had said something about Becca being so good with horses, and Ken had agreed. Merv continued by saying he thought Becca should do something again the next summer in the area of horses, either in Pennsylvania or Indiana, and Ken had looked at Becca as if to say "Well?'

Becca had just said that sounded good, but she didn't know.

And then it got more intense. Merv told Ken that his parents had been Amish years ago, but left when he was a child. He said he had a lot of respect for the Amish—after all, he made his living as an "Amish taxi"—but occasionally he got to know someone he felt just wouldn't ever really fit into the Amish mold. And Becca is one of those, he'd said, smiling at her. He'd asked Ken if he agreed, and Ken's answer was that he'd certainly encourage Becca to consider her options in life and not to assume anything at this age.

The whole conversation frustrated her a lot, and although they asked her questions, it seemed she was being talked about as if she wasn't even there. She had to hand it to Ken, though; he wasn't nearly as pushy as Merv seemed to be. While Merv seemed determined to help Becca leave the Amish, Ken came across more as wanting her to know she had a variety of opportunities in her life, and some of those meant being Amish and some didn't.

In the end, it was Ken who threw the zinger in — the one that still had her shaking her head in disbelief. "I guess it'll be between her and God, won't it?" he'd said, looking directly at Merv and then Becca. The comment had pretty well shut Merv up, and Becca was thankful. As much as she liked him, she was beginning to resent the pressure he was putting on her.

The words may have quieted Merv, but they incited a storm within Becca. What in the world was that supposed to mean?

And so she tossed in her bed, the heavy humid night outside matched by the burden in her soul. When Becca finally slept, she escaped to dream of Al and the carefree excitement of dancing the two-step.

Chapter 15

al

In September, a soggy gray blanket draped itself over Gary County and much of Pennsylvania, creating a seemingly perpetual state of rain, almost-rain, and fog. When the fog rolled into the valleys at night and still sat there in the early morning light, Becca wondered what woud happen in ninety days. If her father's weather predictions held true, Gary County could look forward to mountains of snow in December. She was glad she'd be back in Kansas by then.

For that matter, she'd be ready to go any day, especially if the depressing grayness didn't lift soon. The occasional peek of the sun between clouds was only enough to reassure everyone that it still existed, but Becca needed more. She needed days and days of sunshine. It didn't help that Ken had gone to college the first of September, and she didn't have him to talk to. And it didn't help that business wasn't as strong in September. Becca got to the point where she didn't ever want to see another pillow or hand towel, quilt or quillo again. She knew many Amish women enjoyed making them, but the fine work drove her crazy. She only did it to keep busy, to pass the time, and for the potential income. Not that they were selling much now either, but the inventory for the future was certainly growing.

The last day of September, a pale, watery, half-drowned sun climbed over the horizon in the morning and refused to go away all day. Becca found work to do outdoors, just to be there. When she saw the mail carrier stop at the Beiler mailbox at the end of the lane, she left the garden and sprinted to the mailbox, running for the sheer joy of it. Maybe she'd get a letter, maybe she wouldn't. She just needed to run in the sun.

"Becca Bontrager." Her mother's neat inscription jumped out at her from one of the white envelopes in the stack of mail. She continued flipping through the letters, but it was the only one for her. She read it as she walked slowly back to the yard.

The letter was fairly long, full of the usual news, comings and goings of the family. Only one part made Becca stop and read it again.

> *Since you said you wanted to stay there for some weddings in October, we've done some checking to see if there's a van going up for any of them. It looks like there'll be at least one van load coming the last weekend in October, so we're planning on you catching a ride back with them unless something else comes up. We sure are looking forward to seeing you again!*

So, she was going home in a month, in a van full of Amish kids. That sounded like a lot of fun, Becca smiled. She wondered who would be in the van.

As if determined to make up for lost time, the sun turned October into a glorious month of bright days and colors. The annual pilgrimage of Fall Foliage bus tours, most of them consisting of retired people, crawled through the small towns and countryside of Gary County. Becca loved the beautiful trees, the briskness of the fall air, and the busyness at Beilers Buggy Rides. Plus, she was going to several all-day weddings. The weeks flew by, and before she knew it, the last weekend in October was just a few days away.

Tuesday of that week, she was returning with yet another ooh-ing and ahh-ing couple on a buggy ride when Becca saw something that almost made her stop in the middle of the explanation she was giving about Amish weddings. She hadn't even turned into the Beiler lane yet, but she could see it clearly from the road — a bright red Ford pickup sat in front of the house. She knew that pickup. It could only belong to one person. Al!

Chapter
15

Becca had a terrible time concentrating on the conversation in the buggy as Socks took them down the lane and toward the house. She could see Al's tall slender figure leaning against his pickup, watching the buggy come down the lane. He had on a black cowboy hat — she could see that. As they drew closer, she noticed the huge western belt buckle at his trim waist, and he was wearing a green western shirt, black jeans, and shiny black boots. He grinned at her — a cocky, are-you-surprised-to-see-me-or-what kind of grin. She beamed back and waved.

As soon as the couple was out of the buggy and walking to the quilt store, Al strode toward Becca.

"Excuse me, ma'am," he said with an exaggerated drawl, "I drove all the way from Kansas for a buggy ride. Do you 'spose you could find it in your heart to give me one?"

Becca blushed and giggled, and her dark eyes teased the newcomer.

"It'll cost you a lot, and you have to pay up front," she answered.

"No problem — name your price," Al said, and pulled a wallet out of his back pocket. He started opening it, then paused. "On second thought, I think you're going to be the one owing me, seein's as how I'm taking you back to Kansas. And that's a much longer ride, I do believe."

"What? Really? I thought I was riding with a van load of kids. At least that's what Mom wrote me."

"That was before the van filled up, and I decided to drive out myself."

"And Mom and Dad said it was okay?"

"Hey, you still think they don't trust me? And after I spend the whole summer getting them to like me? Come on! Give me a break!" Al said, feigning disgust, but Becca knew better.

"Is that why you kept asking about me? They'd write and say 'Al's been asking about you.' But did I ever hear from this Al who was supposedly asking about me?" Becca pushed him playfully in the shoulder and answered her own question, "NO!"

"Hey!" Al said, and grabbed Becca's hand that had pushed him, then took the other one too. "I'm not the letter-writin' type."

"Obviously," Becca commented, pretending to struggle for just a moment, then gave in to the feeling of Al holding her hands, standing so close. "I guess this makes up for it though."

Neither one moved for a second, and Becca had to wonder what might have happened next if it hadn't been the middle of the day in the center of the Beiler yard. The thought of being in the dark somewhere with Al, with those same sparks flying between them, made her knees wobbly. She trembled to think how his kiss would feel on her lips.

"Well, you probably need to be giving rides," Al said, breaking the spell, dropping her hands. "I'm gonna run around and check some things out, and I'll be back later this evening. That is, if you wanna go into town for ice cream or something."

"I'd love to," Becca said. "I'll see you later."

It wasn't until then that she noticed a trio of older

women had come out of the quilt store and were patiently waiting for a ride. Her face flushed and her hands unusually nervous, she helped them step into the buggy.

Al came back that evening, and the next too. Thursday was the day of the wedding he'd come for, and he picked Becca up and took her along. The groom was Al's second cousin, and Becca knew the couple because they were friends of Barbara's.

This was Becca's third wedding to attend in as many weeks, and she knew what to expect. The morning was spent sitting on hard backless benches, listening to sermons, just like church. Finally, around noon, the wedding couple would be asked to stand before the bishop and exchange vows. Everyone and everything was very serious and somber. Becca had lots of time to let her mind wander, and an interesting thought crossed her consciousness. If English people, like Leonard's family, could have a funeral that celebrated his life and included smiles and warm feelings, what must their weddings be like? Surely they would be very different too. She wished she could see one.

Not that Amish weddings didn't have lots of celebration and good times, she smiled slightly to herself as she sat next to Barbara during the wedding. Beginning with the huge meal at noon and continuing with the gift opening, singing, visiting, and another meal for the young folks in the evening, the good times flowed freely. That was the "official" part of the wedding. What "flowed freely" among the young folks out in the barn, beside buggies and pickups was an equally expected although certainly less accepted part of the wedding atmosphere. Becca wondered what it would be like to be with Al at a post-wedding party.

She found out later that evening. A large group of

young people had gathered in the huge barn on the farm where the wedding was held. Al himself had a good-sized audience, listening to him tell stories about weddings he had been to and crazy things that had been done to the wedding couple.

He's got an audience that's never heard or seen him before, Becca realized. *The guys are intrigued with his personality and his stories, and the girls can't keep their eyes off of him. He's eating this up.*

He was drinking too. As were many of the kids. By the time the party started to wind down, Al's words were slurring. He sauntered toward Becca, who'd been hanging out with a group of girls most of the evening.

"Time to get in my bug-gy ... and take you back to ... Beilers," he said, smiling crookedly at Becca. "You ready ... to go?"

"You don't have a buggy here, and you're in no condition to drive your pickup," Becca answered. "We'd be better off with *me* driving *you* tonight."

Al seemed to think about that for a minute, then responded. "I was chust callin' my pickup a buggy, ya know what I mean? Naw, I don't think ya should drive it."

"Well, neither should you," Becca replied.

"Hm...mm...mm. What we gonna do then?" Al asked, and put his arm around Becca's waist and murmured into her ear.

A strange mixture of attraction and revulsion flooded Becca. Yes, this was the same Al whose kisses the two nights before had ignited a passion new and powerful in her. But this Al smelled of alcohol, and his words in her ear burned with a different kind a fire — a fire that scared her. She slowly pulled away.

"I'll be right back," she said. "Gotta go, but I'll be right back." She walked away quickly, knowing she had to think of something, come up with some sort of plan.

When she returned, Al was sound asleep behind the wheel of his pickup. Becca quietly pulled the keys from the ignition and took them with her into the house. She'd find a place to lie down there for the few hours left of the night.

129

Chapter
15

"If I was a real jerk, I'm sorry," Al said the next evening, staring straight ahead at the Pennsylvania turnpike. "We've got too many miles ahead of us for you to be mad at me the whole time."

"That's true," Becca said. "And yes, you were a jerk."

"Well, I'm sorry. Forgive me?" Al asked, and reached over to take Becca's hand.

Becca turned to look at him, and waited until Al's eyes left the road and met hers. Any hint of teasing or cocky self-confidence was gone — they were sincere eyes, she figured.

"Okay, apology accepted. But don't let it happen again."

Al didn't answer for awhile, and when he did, he looked at Becca so honestly and so long she got nervous about him not watching the road.

"Here's the truth. I may party now, and I may do stupid things. When I find the girl I want to go steady with, I'll be good. And," Al's eyes returned to the road, and a grin to his face, "and when I find that girl and choin the church and settle down, I'm gonna be one heck of a good husband and father."

Somehow, Becca believed him.

Chapter 16

Home

Becca hadn't realized, until Al's pickup was about a mile from her home, how much she'd missed her family and their Kansas farm. For several hours already, she'd been absorbing and appreciating the wide expanse of sky, the ability to see the horizon, and the space between towns and farms and cities. Yes, it felt good to be in Kansas. And now, as they drew near the Bontrager farm, her heart quickened at the thought of seeing her family again. This is stupid, she thought. No it's not, she heard another part of her say. You've been gone five months! You have every right to be excited!

They pulled into the yard Sunday afternoon, and the pickup hadn't stopped before the back door opened and five eager Bontragers spilled out onto the yard. A cold north wind hit Becca as she opened the pickup door and stepped down, but she hardly noticed. It's hard to notice the wind when you're completely surrounded by a family hug, she thought from somewhere in the middle of the pack.

Jonas, Sue Ann, Lydianne, E.J. and Emma finally pulled away, and Jonas strode over to the pickup to talk to Al. E.J. asked Becca if he could bring in her suitcase, and she said sure, it was in the back of the truck. Sue Ann had her arm around Becca and didn't seem to want to let go, and Lydianne just seemed happy to have her sister back home. And Emma … Emma was the one Becca couldn't believe.

Emma hadn't been walking when Becca left for Pennsylvania, and now she toddled on her short stout legs wherever she wanted to go. She seemed less of a baby and more a little person — one who was understanding and responding much more than she had before. Becca crouched down and called her name, reaching out her arms to Emma. Emma stood looking at her, and then with a grin and a giggle, baby-ran into Becca's arms.

And speaking of growing, E.J. must have added several inches in height over the summer, Becca thought, looking up from where she was hugging Emma. He *had* turned eleven while she was gone, and he seemed less boyish and more mature.

The family chattered its way into the house with Jonas bringing up the rear. He'd asked Al if he wanted to come in for a bit after the long drive, but Al had declined, saying he just wanted to get home, take a shower, and crash. He hadn't said any sort of special good-bye to Becca in front of her family, and she was glad for that.

"Did you have a good trip?" Sue Ann asked, once they were in the house.

"Yeah, it was okay, but not as comfortable as in the train," Becca answered.

"When did you leave? Did you stop for the night?"

"We left Friday late afternoon, drove until midnight, and stopped. Then we drove all day yesterday and stopped last night too. Al needed to get some sleep."

"The question is, did he get some sleep?" Lydianne whispered loud enough for Becca to hear but just out of Sue Ann's earshot.

Becca made a fist and pretended to threaten her sister, who just laughed. The exchange didn't escape Sue Ann's eyes, but all she said was, "I'm just so glad you're home safe and sound."

It felt good to be home, Becca couldn't deny that. But after the initial excitement was over, and she'd told everything she could remember or wanted her family to know about her time in Pennsylvania, she quickly fell back into the routine. Help with the outside chores, help with the household tasks, take care of Emma — the rituals didn't change much. She lived for the weekends when she could escape and be gone — gone with the young folks.

The weekends should be enough to carry her through the weeks, she thought, and at first, they did. She spent time with Al, but neither of them was ready to go steady with each other. They'd talked about it on the drive from Pennsylvania to Kansas, and Becca said when it came right down to it, she felt too young to be going steady at 16. Al, on the other hand, knew he was ready when the right girl came along, and went so far as to say that Becca might be the right one. But he respected the fact that she was four years younger than he, and they decided not to make any commitments toward each other for the time being.

Becca had been home a little over a month when, while hanging the family laundry outdoors on a sharply cold December day, she was reminded of hanging the laundry on the tall line between the Beilers house and barn. That memory brought back thoughts of the evening Ken came over and they ended up going for a walk. She'd thought of Ken often since he'd gone to college, and wondered how he was doing. But it wasn't until that moment that she realized what she was missing in her life. She was missing the talks they'd had.

Sure, she could talk with Lydianne about guys and

such, and what was going on with the young folks. But she didn't have anyone to talk to about the questions Merv had raised at the restaurant that evening. She didn't have anyone to say "Becca, think about this," or "Becca, what do you want out of life?" She only had young people around her who seemed determined to have as much fun as they could before they assumed the harness of Amish life, and parents who seemed happy and satisfied in that role. Until Merv started asking questions and Ken encouraged her to think for herself, she would have probably been in the same position. But now … now the questions lay in the back of her mind and she didn't know what to do with them.

Becca hung the last pair of gray wool socks on the line and picked up the laundry basket. As she walked back to the house, she realized what she needed. She needed to talk to Ken. It wasn't as if he was thousands of miles away either. They'd looked it up on the map before he left — his college was in Marlow, about two hours away from Wellsford. They'd exchanged addresses too, just in case one of them wanted to write the other. Ken hadn't written her, and she hadn't really expected him to. He was probably busy with college classes and activities. But now she was going to write him. Yes, that's what she'd do.

Later that day, after supper and the dishes were done, Becca retreated to her room. She lit the lamp on her dresser and took a box of stationery out of one of the drawers.

> *Dear Ken,*
>
> *How are you? You're probably having a good time at college, and don't even remember me. I'm the gal with the 12 kids who makes you carry her groceries.*

Becca drew a big happy face after that sentence, then continued.

You missed a very dreary September in Pennsylvania when you went to college, but then October was just as beautiful as September was nasty. We were busy with the rides, plus weddings to go to. Al showed up the last week in October for a wedding and I went home with him.

Boy, that doesn't say much, Becca thought, flicking her pen back and forth in her hand absentmindedly. But it's hard to write all of that down. It'd be so much easier just to talk.

It was neat to come back home again, especially to see how E.J. and Emma have changed. Other than that, not much has changed. I'm doing what I did before I left — chores, laundry, meals, cleaning.

Becca put another face after that sentence, but this time the mouth turned down.

I have to admit, I'm secretly hoping I can go back again next summer. I love Kansas, and I don't like it as much in Gary County as far as there being so many people and everything. But I love giving the rides, and there just isn't anything like that a girl can do around here. I hope my parents will let me go. That's the last thing Amos said to me before I left — he said he sure hoped I'd be back next summer.

The other thing I miss about Gary County is talking to you.

There, she'd said it. She pondered her next words, then wrote:

I guess there was just something about the way we

could talk about anything. You helped me think about a lot of things, and you opened my mind to ideas I'd never thought of before. Remember the day we were walking past the Beilers Buggy Rides sign, and you stopped and said, "Who knows, someday you could have a sign that says Becca's Buggy Rides"? That blew me away. I'd never dreamed of that possibility, but you said dreams can come true if you make the right choices along the way and you work to make it happen.

 I also remember how, at the restaurant with Merv and Ella, you said something about it being between me and God if I was going to leave or stay with the Amish. What does that mean? We never talked about it because you left for college a few days later.

 I wish we could get together sometime.

Becca paused again. Was she being too forward? Oh well, what did she have to lose?

 I don't know if it would ever work for you to come here, but that would be neat. It'd be fun to catch up with each other. I hope you're doing okay.
 Sincerely, Becca

The hopefulness Becca had felt while waiting for a letter from Al that summer paled in comparison to the way she opened the Bontrager mailbox for the next week. Her sudden interest in getting the mail didn't bypass Sue Ann or Lydianne. Becca could feel their eyes watching as she put on her coat every day to run to the mailbox and as she returned, but neither of them said anything. She knew Sue Ann was very curious but trying to respect her privacy. She'd shared enough with Lydianne about her friendship with Ken that

Lydianne probably suspected who she was hoping to hear from.

The day the letter came, Becca tried to act nonchalant as she deposited the family mail on the kitchen table and then ran up the stairs to her room, carrying a white envelope. She could hear Lydianne's giggling in the kitchen, and Sue Ann's questioning voice. She didn't really care if Lydianne told Sue Ann.

Becca read from the white sheet of notebook paper.

> *Dear Becca,*
>
> *I'm sitting in my History of Religion class, and the lecture is kinda boring today, so I think I'll write you instead. It was good to hear from you! I've often thought about how you're doing. I figured you're having lots of fun with the young folks during the weekends, and recuperating during the week. But you didn't say much about that in your letter. So either you aren't having much fun, or you're having so much, you're embarrassed to tell me about it.*

Ken had drawn a happy face after that sentence, and Becca smiled.

> *You're right about me being busy with things here at college, but I'm really enjoying it. I'm taking accounting classes that will help me with the store, and the Bible and Religion classes are, for the most part, quite interesting. You'd be amazed at some of the discussions we have.*
>
> *In fact, here's an idea. One of our classes that is studying different religions has been going to visit a variety of churches. Would there be any chance of us coming to visit one of your worship services? I know*

that might not be possible, and if not, do you think your father would be willing to talk to them about some of the basics of the Amish religion? I think there would be about 30 of us.

Maybe it's a crazy idea, but I know the class would love it. If that happened, it probably wouldn't give you and me very much time to talk, unless I drove up by myself or the carload I was in decided to stay around a little longer. I guess we'll deal with that when I hear from you about the possibility of us coming.

Well, class is over, so I'd better quit. I know this isn't very long, but maybe I can do better next time.

Bye for now,
Ken

Becca lay back on her bed and stared up at the ceiling. Ken wanted to bring a class of college students to their house to hear her father talk about the Amish religion. Asking her father would mean admitting her friendship with Ken. That was the first problem. She remembered Jonas's letter after Leonard's funeral. If he was scared then about her leaving, how would he feel now? And would he even consider talking to students who had so much more education than he?

All she'd wanted was to talk to Ken, and now look what he'd gotten her into. Becca sighed and stuck the letter back into the envelope.

Chapter 17
God's Bridle

Becca still couldn't quite believe it. She didn't know why he'd said yes, but there stood her father in the family living room, talking to more than thirty college students and their professor. The students sat on the couch, on chairs, on the floor, listening intently to Jonas's description of what it meant to be Amish, and why they believed what they did. The bright January sunshine poured into the windows around the group, and Becca was glad for the mild weather that weekend. Ken had been worried that a winter storm would prevent the class from making the trip at the last minute, but even the weather seemed to want to cooperate.

Jonas had been talking for about twenty minutes, and Becca was surprised at how relaxed he appeared. But then, she realized, this was no different from standing up and giving a sermon every Sunday. Sure, he was addressing people he didn't know with a lot more education than he had. But he knew his subject well, and unlike many of the Amish people who occasionally dozed off during the long service, this audience was all ears. Her father was a good speaker, and they were eating it up.

The class was asking the usual questions — many which Becca had become accustomed to answering while giving buggy rides. Were Amish and Mennonites the same? Why the strict rules against cars and electricity and so many other things? What were their basic beliefs? Did they lose a lot of people to "the world"? Why didn't they have church buildings? Why didn't they allow their pictures to be taken? What was the structure of their religious organization? Of each individual church?

Becca listened intently. Although she knew most of the answers, at least the abbreviated version, she'd never heard her father explain them at length to anyone. Sure, there had been explanations when she asked questions as a child, but it was different now. She was a young adult who found herself understanding some of the explanations and questioning others.

The Amish and Mennonites were not the same, Jonas had answered, although they shared common ancestors prior to a split back in the late 1600s. To this day, they shared the practices of adult baptism and nonresistance with the Mennonites, but other than that, the Mennonites were more progressive or worldly than the Amish. Becca knew from her summer in Pennsylvania that there were a number of different Mennonite and Amish groups, with the Old Order Amish being the most conservative.

Jonas went on to explain that separation from the world is a fundamental aspect of Amish religion — a belief that came from the biblical teaching to be separate from the world. In order to survive as a people, the Amish separate themselves from the modern things that, over time, could destroy their close-knit communities. Ownership of a car, for example, gives the owner freedom to go much farther than a horse and buggy. Having a telephone in the home makes the family a slave to its ringing, and interrupts family time. Going somewhere else to use a phone is different because they are in control of the phone, not the phone controlling them.

No, Jonas said, the Amish don't lose a lot of people to

the world. The temptations of the world may be attractive, but they don't carry much weight when stacked against the love of family, the security of belonging to a close-knit group, and the belief that those who are born Amish are meant to stay Amish.

Jonas continued talking, but Becca's concentration was stuck on his words about not losing people to the world. The love of family ... security ... those who are born are meant to stay. She shifted in her chair uneasily. Then one of the class members asked a question that caught her attention again.

"Did you ever consider leaving?"

Jonas stood, studying the floor for awhile, and Becca could guess what was going on inside of him. It was one thing to answer general questions about Amish beliefs. It was another thing entirely to share about his personal life.

Finally Jonas cleared his throat and said, "Yes. When I was a teenager. Fortunately, and I will always be grateful to Sue Ann for this," Jonas looked over to where Sue Ann was standing against the wall in the corner, "Sue Ann helped me to see that being Amish and living the simple life is both who we are and what we are called by God to do."

The questions continued, including some about the church organization and how Jonas became a minister. Becca listened as intently as the others as Jonas described what had happened the day he was made minister and how that had felt to him. She'd been eight at the time, but she hadn't been in the room when Jonas and five other men sat in front of the congregation, each opening a songbook to see whose book held the slip of paper — the slip that would make the man minister for life. The lot had hit Jonas, and after the initial shock, he'd adjusted well to his new role within the church.

As Becca listened to her father talk, she felt a sense of

warm appreciation growing in her heart for what he was doing. She knew not many Amish people would share as freely and openly as he was, nor would they all be able to express the whys and wherefores of what they believed. Yes, her father was quite a man.

Finally, the class professor said they'd taken more than enough of Jonas's time, and they'd need to be going. Everyone thanked Jonas over and over, and he said he was glad he could do it. As the group began getting their coats and heading toward the door, Ken and Becca's eyes connected and they managed to find their way to each other in the room.

"I'm sorry it didn't work for me to stay longer this time," Ken apologized. "But I have another idea."

"Oh boy, another one of your ideas," Becca said teasingly.

"I think you'll like it, if it works out," Ken said, smiling back. "We're going to have a Christian music festival on campus in two weeks. I was wondering if you'd like to go. I'd come pick you up and you could spend the night in the girls dorm with some girls I know. Then I'd bring you back the next day. That should give us some time to talk and catch up with each other, plus I think you'd love the concerts."

Becca's eyes shone "YES!" for several moments before they clouded and she said, "I'm going to have to ask my parents. After what Dad said today about those who are born Amish are meant to stay Amish ..."

"Yeah, I know," Ken agreed. "But it can't hurt to try, can it?"

"I'll let you know," Becca said.

Despite her fear that he would say no, Becca decided to

approach her father first, alone. She'd always been able to relate to him a little better than to her mother. She decided to catch him during chores that evening if possible.

"Dad, I need to talk to you," she said as Jonas walked into the horse barn that evening. She'd lucked out — she was feeding the horses alone and Jonas had just happened to come in for something.

"Yes?"

"Why did you agree to do that talk to those students?"

Jonas gave her a puzzled look before answering. "I guess I didn't see any reason not to."

"You know that it's because I'm friends with Ken that he had the idea to come here. To bring the class, I mean," she hastily added.

"Yes, I know that."

"Aren't you mad about that?"

Jonas picked a piece of straw out of a bale and began chewing on it. "Becca, I cannot be with you all of the time, telling you who you can have as friends. Of course I'm concerned about this. Like I said in that letter, you are starting to make choices that will affect the rest of your life. Your mom and I have done the best we can in raising you, and we're still trying to give you guidance. But we can't keep you in a prison here."

"Remember when we stood in this barn years ago, and you told me you were going to sell Preacher?" Becca asked, searching her father's face.

"Yes, I do."

"Did you sell Preacher because something inside of you told you to do that?"

"Yes."

"Was that something God?"

It was Jonas's turn to study his daughter's eyes.

"Yes, I think it was, because the next day I got made minister."

"And if there are going to be some Christian music concerts at Menno Simons college, and Ken wants to pick me up and take me to them, and I feel like something inside of me is telling me to do that, could that be God too?"

"Becca, I don't know. It sounds more like something *you* want to do."

"But when do we know it's what we want and when do we know it's God?"

"That's a big question, Becca, and it doesn't have any easy answers."

"What about me going? Would you let me?"

Jonas sat down on the bale of straw and studied the floor. When he lifted his head, Becca saw pain and indecision in his eyes.

"I could say no, and then you'd be mad at me, and it wouldn't stop you from having those outside influences in your life, one way or the other. Or I could say yes, and maybe you'll go and enjoy those worldly things, like I did, and come back, like I did. Or maybe, because of Ken or somebody or something else, you'll decide someday that you like it out there more than you value our faith and tradition. Then I will be angry at myself."

Becca sat down next to her father. "Dad, you know I love you, and you know I wouldn't do anything just for the sake of making you mad. And you know that it wouldn't be your fault if I wouldn't be Amish. That would be my choice, not your responsibility."

"But I would feel very responsible," Jonas said. "Although I'm beginning to realize that the only thing I can do is hope and pray that you will find the right way."

"And when you pray, will you be telling God what's the right way?"

A flare of passion streaked Jonas's eyes and face, and Becca was afraid. She hadn't meant to anger her father, but

the question just came out. She certainly didn't want to be disrespectful to her father or to God.

Jonas stood up and walked to the other end of the horse barn. He slowly lifted a horse bridle from where it was hanging on the wall and brought it back to where Becca was still seated on the bale. He sat down beside her.

"Becca," her father began, "a horse or mule isn't much good around here if he refuses to wear a bridle. You can't guide him — for driving the buggy, or working in the field, or riding. He isn't useful, and he doesn't have a purpose for being here."

"People are the same, Becca. Wearing God's bridle gives us direction and purpose. I believe that bridle, for me, is being Amish, and I believe with my whole heart that you and I belong on the same team."

Jonas paused, rubbing the bridle with his hand.

"The most important thing, Becca, is that you wear God's bridle. And if for some reason you and I end up on different teams, I don't know that I will understand it, but I do know I will always love you because you are my daughter."

"And I will always love you, Dad," Becca cried, wrapping her arms around her father. He smelled of the outdoors, and livestock, and his beard tickled her neck. She felt his strong arms wrap around her in return, and she knew. She knew what he said was true.

THE END

COMING NEXT:

Follow Becca's life in

TWINS

Book 1 in the Skye Series

The Authors

Husband-and-wife authors Maynard Knepp and Carol Duerksen share their farm between Goessel and Hillsboro, Kansas, with exchange students and a variety of animals. Maynard grew up Amish near Yoder, Kansas, and manages a hog facility near Hutchinson. Carol is a full-time freelance writer. They are active members of Tabor Mennonite Church near Goessel.

The Illustrator

Susan Bartel has illustrated several books and many magazine stories. She lives with her husband and two children at Rocky Mountain Mennonite Camp near Divide, Colorado.

Would you like the other books in the Jonas Series?
How about buying some as gifts for family and friends?
• •

Order Form

Please send _____ copy/copies of *Runaway Buggy* @ $9.95 each

_____ copy/copies of *Hitched* @ $9.95 each

_____ copy/copies of *Preacher* @ $9.95 each

_____ copy/copies of *Becca* @ $9.95 each

Name _____

Address _____

City _____ State _____

Zip _____ Phone # _____

_____ Book(s) at $9.95 = Total $ _____

Add $3 postage/handling if only one copy _____

SPECIAL PRICE = Buy 2 or more,
pay $10 each and we'll pay the shipping.

Total enclosed $ _____

Make checks payable to WillowSpring Downs and mail,
along with this order form, to the following address:

WillowSpring Downs
Route 2, Box 31
Hillsboro, KS 67063-9600

Any questions or requests for more information can be faxed to:
(316) 367-8218

Would you like the other books in the Jonas Series?
How about buying some as gifts for family and friends?

● ●

Order Form

Please send _____ copy/copies of *Runaway Buggy* @ $9.95 each

_____ copy/copies of *Hitched* @ $9.95 each

_____ copy/copies of *Preacher* @ $9.95 each

_____ copy/copies of *Becca* @ $9.95 each

Name _____

Address _____

City _____ State _____

Zip _____ Phone # _____

_____ Book(s) at $9.95 = Total $ _____

Add $3 postage/handling if only one copy _____

SPECIAL PRICE = Buy 2 or more,
pay $10 each and we'll pay the shipping.

Total enclosed $ _____

Make checks payable to WillowSpring Downs and mail,
along with this order form, to the following address:

WillowSpring Downs
Route 2, Box 31
Hillsboro, KS 67063-9600

Any questions or requests for more information can be faxed to:
(316) 367-8218